No Light Tomorrow
Illustrated Edition

Enjoy the Book!

Mars Lives

[signature]

Thanks and remember,
Nothing is assured!

[signature]

No Light Tomorrow
Illustrated Edition

Christian Laforet
Ben Van Dongen

No Light Tomorrow
Illustrated Edition
AdventureWorldsPress.com

First Printing. September 2016

Published By
Adventure Worlds Press
Windsor Ontario

Edited by Kate Richards
Cover Photo: Cody Maisonneuve
Illustrations by Nikita Why

As Big As Love Previously on AdventureWorldsPress.com

Library and Archives Canada Cataloguing in Publication

Laforet, Christian, author
        No Light Tomorrow Illustrated Edition / Christian Laforet, Ben
Van Dongen.

Science fiction short stories.
ISBN 978-1-987976-20-5 (paperback)

        I. Van Dongen, Ben, 1981-, author II. Title.

Christian Laforet

For Delilah Sunshine
The little girl with the heart of a dragon.

———————

Ben Van Dongen

For my Parents

The Doubling

The Doubling
Christian Laforet

Bob leaned close to the window. He watched the countryside roll past, the blur of green cutting through his reflection. The forecast called for rain, and already, the tumultuous sky peppered the train with drops. He craned his neck to peer up at the grey vista. The clouds hung like a shroud, blocking the sun completely.

He felt like garbage. He hadn't eaten a proper meal in weeks and couldn't remember his last decent night's sleep. Even buying the train ticket had developed into a faded moment, a memory indistinguishable from the events surrounding it. Everything in the last week bled together in his mind.

Lost in thought, he startled at the sudden realization there was a person standing in the aisle beside him.

"Um…is this seat taken?"

He turned to see a young woman. She was pointing towards the empty seat next to him. "Oh, uh, no, go ahead."

The woman smiled and sat down. "Thanks, I wasn't expecting the train to be this full."

"No problem." He was not happy for the company. It distracted him from his thoughts. He hoped the woman would put on headphones or take a nap. She fiddled with her purse for a bit before pulling a rolled-up magazine from within. Bob took it to be a good sign. Hopefully, she would leave him alone.

"Excuse me," the woman asked, as she gently touched his arm. "You seem really familiar. Are you on TV or something?"

He suppressed a groan. Even after ten years, people still recognized him. "Nope. You must be thinking of somebody else." He could tell by the look in her eye she was not going to let that be the end of it.

"Oh…huh, I guess. It's just that, I swear I've seen you somewhere before."

"Well, you're wrong. I'm nobody."

The woman nodded but continued to stare. "Wait! Are you…? Are you one of the Doubled?" The excitement in her voice was undeniable.

There it was. He sighed and tried to twist even farther from the woman.

"You are! I knew I recognized you! That is so crazy. I just watched the Dateline special about the Doubling last week. I can't believe it's already been ten years."

He let out a series of fake coughs before telling the woman he needed to use the washroom. She stood up so he could pass. When she opened her mouth to speak, he coughed some more.

As he moved along the unsteady train, he couldn't help but meet every set of eyes along the way. How many other people had seen that Dateline? How many, right now, were sending messages to family and friends, reading, 'You won't believe who's on this train with me.'

The last few steps to the bathroom were the hardest. Bob wanted to run, but knew that would draw even more attention. He once again cursed his decision to take public transportation for this portion of the trip. Too many potential witnesses.

He stepped into the cramped space of the train's washroom and locked the door behind him. A sigh of relief passed his lips before he reached out and turned on the tap. He cupped his hands, letting the water pool in his palms before splashing it on his face. The cold felt nice, refreshing. Taking a steadying breath, he stared into the mirror.

***

It started like any other Tuesday. His wife, Elle, woke up early and got ready for work while he changed Hannah's diaper and heated her morning bottle. By the time the baby finished her milk, Elle was dressed, leaving Bob free to hop in the shower.

"Can you drop Hannah off at daycare?" Elle asked. "I have to go in early to set up the stats for the housing board presentation."

"Sure."

"Awesome! Love you." She planted a kiss on his forehead. He, in return, patted her rear as she walked away.

"Hey now, none of that." Her mock scolding was accompanied with a wink.

"Oh, c'mon. I hear your husband's a total loser, madam, and that you're in the market for a real man," he said, puffing out his chest.

Elle smiled. "Well, you heard right, sir. Maybe tonight, if my sad excuse for a husband doesn't come home, I can show you my bedroom."

***

While loading Hannah into the car seat, Bob waved to Elle as she backed out of the driveway and disappeared up the road. He knew her first stop would be the Tim Hortons down on Fifth and Maple. The woman couldn't make it until noon without her morning coffee. Bob cracked open an energy drink, his preferred form of caffeine.

The day was nice, sunny but cool. Bob pulled into the daycare parking lot. Even though he and Elle called it a daycare, the large sign posted over the front of the building insisted it was actually a school dedicated to early childhood education. As far as he was concerned, it was a daycare.

Although Elle usually dropped their daughter off, it wasn't completely unusual for him to do it. Walking through the squat structure, he exchanged polite greetings with several women who worked there. He wasn't sure of their names, but saw them often enough to give a friendly smile.

Hannah's classroom was located near the back of the building. Bob talked to one of the three women responsible for the children in the room before sitting his daughter on the padded floor next to a pile of multi-coloured blocks. The woman—he was pretty sure her name was Ada—waved goodbye and assured him they would take good care of Hannah.

The moment he stepped out the front door, Bob knew something was wrong. The beautiful blue sky was now a sickly green. The air, comfortably cool earlier, had grown downright cold and very dry. A shiver raced along his body, leaving an uncomfortable feeling clinging to him. There was something else in the air, besides the chill—it felt charged.

A strong, unexplained need to get out of the open space of the parking lot urged him towards his car. Reaching a hand into his pocket in search of his keys, he noticed his fingertips tingling. It was an odd sensation—like pins and needles. The feeling spread through his body. When it reached his head, it erupted into a skull-splitting headache. He let out a pained yelp, the fillings in his teeth vibrating.

Above him, the green sky shook. He was mesmerized

by what was happening, despite the piercing pain in his head. The phenomenon extended as far as he could see, leaving him disoriented. He was forced to lean against a nearby silver SUV to keep his balance. The shaking intensified. It was as if the very air around him was being torn asunder. Bob dropped to the asphalt and covered his head with his arms. He could feel the world around him contort and expand. His screaming was quickly gobbled up by a rending din, which culminated in a violent snap. A shock wave of air rippled across the back of his shirt.

Ears ringing, he rose on unsteady legs and stared in awe at the clear blue sky. He was vaguely aware of other people stumbling around the parking lot, but he paid them no mind. His first coherent thought was concern for Hannah.

The front door seemed an almost impossible distance away, especially on rubbery legs. In reality, he'd only walked a few metres from the main entrance before the sky fell. He reached for the door but was cut off as another man beat him to it.

The stranger turned to look at him. Bob was struck dumb. The man was him. He didn't just resemble Bob, he was identical. They were even dressed the same.

He knew the expression on the man's face matched his own: fear. He backed up. His double did the same.

His mind shot through a thousand different questions, all of them with impossible answers. The stranger began to position aggressively in front of him. Bob knew the man was going to attack him, so he beat him to the punch and threw a wild, looping fist, connecting squarely with his jaw. He watched, stunned, as his double tumbled backwards, all but flattening a small bush next to the entrance. He did not wait to see if the man got up. Instead, he yanked the door open and darted into the building.

Inside was a lesson in chaos. Nearly all the adults were

screaming, fighting, or, in two cases, lying unconscious on the linoleum floor. Ada came shrieking down the hall, blowing past him, and slammed into the front door. She hit it so hard that instead of swinging open, the glass panes broke under the pressure and both her arms shot through the shards. A dozen lines appeared on her exposed skin; blood started flowing almost instantly. The woman, somewhat unfazed, simply pushed the smashed door open. She left two bloody handprints along the frame and ran into the parking lot. Moments later, Ada ran past him a second time. This version of the woman repeated the first's mistake, but, lucky for her, the glass was already gone.

Shaking his head, he hurried to his daughter's classroom. He glanced in all the other rooms along the way and saw that not just the adults had been doubled, but the children as well. At least the kids seemed to be taking it much better than their parents and teachers. They simply talked and played with their unexpected twins.

When he entered Hannah's classroom and found two of her rolling around on the padded floor, he slapped a hand over his mouth to stifle the gasp he knew was coming. He instinctively grabbed the Hannah nearest to him and rationalized that he would know his real daughter from some sort of fake.

"Stay the hell away from my little girl!"

Bob twisted to see his copy come running into the room and snap up the other Hannah. The man had a small cut above his eye. A smear of blood arced across his forehead and vanished into his hairline.

The Bob-double jabbed a finger towards him. "I don't know who the fuck you are, or...or what's going on, but you'd better keep your distance!"

Bob couldn't agree more with the other him and had quickly turned to leave, when the cellphone in his pocket began to vibrate. Keeping his eyes on the man across the room, he fished out the device. Only when the phone was directly in front of him did he glance at the screen. Elle's name flashed in time with the vibrations.

"Hello? Elle?" Bob spoke urgently into the cell. He thought his phone was causing an echo, but then noticed his doppelganger was talking into a cellphone of his own. It took him a moment to realize he could hear his double through his phone. They had both connected to the call.

Her voice was very faint. "Bob. I, I don't know…I'm hurt and there's…oh god, I'm bleeding, and there's another… another me."

"Where are you?" he and the other Bob asked in stereo.

With her voice failing her, Elle managed to relay her location before the line went dead.

Bob spun for the door, Hannah held tight in his arms. He knew exactly where Elle was. Once out of the room, he took a moment to topple over a large cabinet located next to the exit. Since the doors opened outwards, it would take his double some heavy pushing to move it. He wasn't entirely sure why he felt the need to hinder the other Bob, but he figured nothing good could come of having the man around.

The world outside was like a war zone. Cars were crashing all over the place. People were running through the streets, screaming. Bodies lay on the sidewalks. It was overwhelming, but he needed to stay focused on his wife. He needed to find Elle.

Clearly, whatever had happened at the daycare had a wider effect than just the small building. Within two blocks his car was completely stuck in gridlocked traffic. Besides the numerous accidents littering the roads, a great many of the cars clogging the streets were abandoned. Leaving his own to join the collection, he unsnapped Hannah from her car seat, picked her up, and started sprinting.

Hannah giggled in his arms as he ran. Bob used the

baby's laugh as an anchor, a weight which would let him ignore the fact he passed two identical dogs pissing on the same fire hydrant, or that two old men lay dead across the street, hands clutching their chests, completely indistinguishable from each other.

Taking great gulps of breath, Bob came to a skidding stop as he rounded the corner of Fifth and Maple. The Tim Hortons located there was fully ablaze. It wasn't just the donut shop, either. Black smears of smoke dirtied the sky in all directions.

An employee from the donut shop shambled past, her uniform burned along the right side, most of her hair singed off. "Was it a car or a cat I saw?" she muttered. Bob waved to get the woman's attention, but she stumbled on down the sidewalk asking her nonsense question.

Elle's car was a block from the Tim's. She had driven off the road. Bob slowed as he neared it, intense fear gripping him. The front end was crumpled against a tall oak tree. Branches and leaves littered the surrounding area.

Pulling Hannah tighter to his chest, Bob approached the vehicle from the passenger side. He let out a horrified moan when he came to the door. The engine had pushed up through the dashboard; twisted steel had reduced the woman sitting in the seat's face to a pulp. He could tell from her clothing and build it was his wife. His knees went weak, and he felt like he was going to faint. As he moved to find support, his perspective shifted. Slightly past the woman, another Elle slumped in the driver's seat, her head tilted back at an awkward angle.

"Elle!" Bob rushed around the back of the car.

Fearing the worst, he slowly reached through the broken driver's side window and caressed his wife's face. A large gash in her neck had sent blood down like a waterfall over her chest, painting the cellphone, still clutched tightly in her hand, crimson. He knew she was dead.

A wild scream yanked Bob away from his grief. He spun around in time to see his double rushing up to the car, the fake Hannah held tight in his arms.

"Leave us alone!" Bob shouted at the imposter.

His twin rushed past, gazed in at the horror inside the vehicle, and collapsed to his knees.

Bob wasn't sure if the man knew which Elle was his, but it didn't matter. Either way, Elle was dead and gone. He stumbled away from the wreck, Hannah cooing in his arms. He looked back once and saw his double was also gone. He half expected the man to appear at his house, but he never did.

***

The event, later called 'The Doubling', was labeled a "time anomaly." For reasons even the smartest people on the planet could not explain, everybody within a twenty kilometre radius—which partially covered Bob's hometown—went back in time thirty seconds. This caused an instant doubling of everybody in the area. As perplexing as the event itself was, what was even stranger was that it didn't repeat. It appeared to be a one-off event.

The doubles, which were identified thanks to trace amounts of radiation resulting from the phenomenon, were taken away by the government. After years of testing, they were set up in a small town on the other side of the country. Although the doubles did not have to stay there, most of them did. It would be a couple of generations before they would be able to call this timeline their own.

***

Bob splashed more water on his face. He hadn't realized how badly he needed a shave. He wondered again what his double would look like. It had been ten years of different living. A lot could happen to a person in ten years.

He returned to his seat. The woman with all the questions had gotten the hint and found another place to sit.

Outside, the rain gained in ferocity and began pelting the window. Hundreds of spots appeared along the pane before being stretched into horizontal lines. Bob's reflection twisted and warped under the magnifying glass of countless raindrops.

He checked his watch. If the train was on schedule, he would be arriving shortly at his destination. From there, he would rent a car and follow the directions he'd printed off before leaving home. He reached into the small carry-on bag tucked at his feet and pulled out a stack of folded papers. When he opened them, the picture of Hannah he had stuck in the middle fell out. He hated leaving her, especially at a time like this, but she would be fine with Elle's parents. He rubbed his thumb and index finger into his eyes. The last three years had been long and painful. They'd taken a toll.

The first signs something was wrong came when Hannah started complaining about burning in her chest. Bob had brushed it off as growing pains, but when it got worse he'd taken her to the doctor. Cardiomyopathy, that's what they called it, but Bob didn't care. He was more hung up on what they said after that. Hannah's illness was severe. They told him it would lead to heart failure and death before she was twenty. The doctors assured him that with a transplant she would be able to live a healthy life. Because of the rarity of her blood type, however, the likelihood of receiving one in time was bleak.

Bob leaned back in his seat, the picture held against his chest. He had already made peace with what he was going to do. There was a person out there, an exact copy of his little girl, who would be a perfect match. Ten years was a long time. Maybe that little girl, having lived a different life, was completely healthy. He was going to find out.

The train station was packed as people crowded the concourse. Bob shuffled along towards the car rental desk but slowed as he noticed a small group staring up at one of the televisions secured to the wall. Splashed across the screen, with Breaking News in bold letters at the top, was an image of a house. Bob stopped and scratched his chin—the house resembled his in-laws' place.

"What's going on?" he asked an old woman at the back of the group.

Keeping her eyes fixed on the television, she spoke over her shoulder. "Some psycho, back east, killed some people."

Bob strained to read the text scrolling across the screen. "Who'd he kill?" He tried to swallow the dread building inside of him, but it didn't work.

"Apparently," the woman finally turned her attention towards him, "he shot an old couple and cut out a little girl's heart."

Slow Hallway

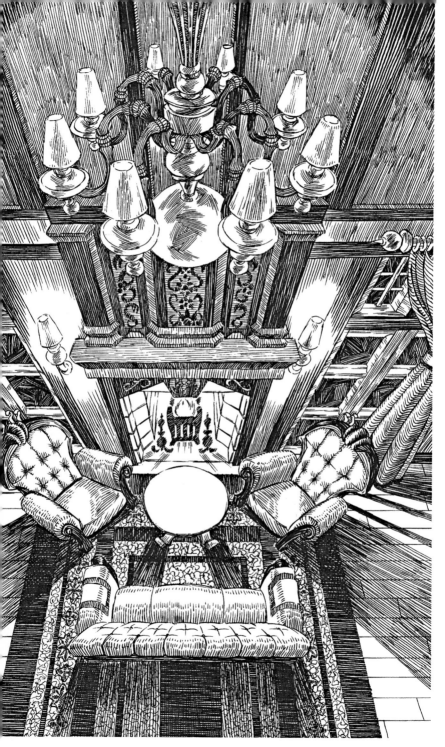

Slow Hallway
Ben Van Dongen

Allen walked up to the over-sized wooden door and pulled the brass handle with a grunt. It didn't move. Taking a step off the stoop, he looked at the old manor-house-turned-hotel. He was in a gated courtyard at the front of the big mansion. The hundred year old building was like something in a Poe story. Ivy crept up the front, pulling at the mortar and wood. The cobblestone courtyard dipped and rolled like a pond with a pebble skipped across it. Every third stone was broken or missing, adding chop to the still water. The building was grand from a distance, but shabby in person. The light of the dropping sun, sitting over the trees at the end of the long driveway, reflected off the windows. There was no sign of anyone around.

Taking hold of the ornate handle again, he gave a more zealous tug, leaning away from it, adding weight rather than straining, in case someone saw. It may have moved, but not enough for him to be sure. Knocking, he stood at the door for a full minute, occasionally peeking in the windows at either side. Following the swoops of the intricate carvings, he tried to decide what to do. He could walk around the grounds, trying to find another way in, or he could call the phone number he'd been given. Eventually he banged hard on the wide door. The sound bounced around the courtyard.

A voice came from the right. "Pull harder."

Allen jumped. He saw a head popping out of a window along the right wall. "I tried." He pulled again to illustrate his point.

"Like, really hard."

Wanting to prove to the man—or the head, as it seemed that's all there was—he had pulled hard and wasn't an idiot, Allen braced his feet, grabbed the handle with both hands and wrenched on it. The large door swung open. Allen lost his grip and fell backwards off the low stoop and onto the broken cobblestone. Before he could get up again, the door closed. He clenched his teeth as he got to his feet.

"That was awesome." The head grinned. "You can try again or you can go to the employee's entrance around the corner." An arm joined the head out the window and pointed to a set of stairs leading out of the courtyard. "I hope you try again."

Allen walked towards the wall and climbed the stairs where the stranger pointed. The full man was there to greet him, holding open a much smaller door.

"I take it you're Allen?" He walked away without waiting for an answer.

"Yeah, I'm supposed to be starting tonight." Allen caught the door before it closed then followed. Broken wood chairs were piled to the side of the small entranceway. Faded wallpaper came down to a wooden rail at Allen's waist and chipped wood panels ran to the floor. The paper was torn and smudged, likely from the chairs and other furniture being hastily carried in and out of the building.

"I'm Don. I'm supposed to be showing you around tonight. Come on in." Don led Allen down a hallway off the entrance and into an office overlooking the courtyard. Like the outside of the manor, the office was filled with faded grandeur. An antique desk, heavily used, sat in the middle of the room. A modern metal filing cabinet against the wall clashed with a wood and glass display next to it, and the chairs facing the front of the desk looked to be the best of what was piled by the door.

Allen saw the window where Don had stuck his head out and huffed, stifling a grimace.

"Should be a quiet night. We only have the two couples and Ronnie."

Allen leaned to peek out the window, splitting his curiosity with the conversation. "Who's Ronnie?"

"He's kind of a renter. He's had the same room for the last couple years. Mostly stays in there, though, so we tend to not bother each other." Don sat behind the desk and motioned for Allen to sit in one of the chairs on the other side. Spinning once in the chair, Don slapped the desk with his palms. "So." He cocked an eyebrow and smiled.

Allen noticed that, from the desk, Don had a clear view of the front steps. "How long were you going to watch me struggle to get in?"

"As long as I did. The door is a little tricky, but you'll get used to it in no time. It only sticks for the first couple inches then it swings wild like that." Don took a long sip from a mug sitting on the desk and checked his watch. "Wow. You're early, aren't you? We can get started if you like."

Allen struggled to keep his eyes from rolling. "Yeah, sure." He was reluctant to drop the topic of the front door but didn't want to make a bad impression on his first day.

Using the desk for leverage, Don got up with a long

grunt. "Great, let's go to the hostess room."

"Hostess?"

"Yeah, the position was originally only for women. They never bothered to change the title, so we're hostesses." Don walked back into the hallway and leaned against the tattered wallpaper. "This was the servants' area. Still is, I guess. I suggest coming in this way. You'll get a key and you can avoid the guests until you start your shift. And we're walking." He kicked away from the wall, leaving a footprint, and led the way down the hall.

At every door they passed, Don pointed and rattled off what was behind it. "The servery is where the chef preps all the meals, but he doesn't like to talk to us so I just stay away. If you're bold enough, you can sneak some pretty epic snacks though." Don made a gun with his hand and a popping sound with his mouth.

"The supply closet is self-explanatory—mops, brooms, sprays, and the like. The alarm's in there, too, but we almost never set it. We don't get a lot of traffic, but there's almost always a guest or two. The stairs here go to the second floor hallway and the caretaker's apartment. Don't use it." Don's entire demeanor changed briefly. He crossed his arms, his face placid.

"Will it wake him?" Allen put his hand on a large rounded knob topping the banister. It came off in his hands. He juggled it, narrowly grabbing hold of it before it hit the floor. He propped it into place and inhaled sharply through his teeth then glanced at Don. He scrutinized the rest of the rickety staircase and thought the wooden death-trap should probably be roped off. It was narrow with large gaps in the wood. A couple of the stairs sloped forward and the whole thing was rough and full of splinters.

Don's face was rigid as stone. "Her—and probably. That's not why though. It just takes too long." He glanced up the steps, sighed, and shed the severity. Shuffling back and pumping his arms like a poorly performed dance move, he spun and continued around a corner through a plain, double-hinged door.

The hallway went to the right, but Don led Allen to a door on the left. "This way to the hostess room." He pulled a set of keys from a clip at his waist and opened the door. He let the keys go, and they zipped back to his belt on a line. "Don't be jealous." He raised an eyebrow, smiling.

An end table at the back of the small room served as a workstation. A set of cubbyholes lining the wall across from a sliver of a window, and a coat rack in a corner, made the room cramped, even for a single person.

"You can leave your stuff in here, get any messages, sign in and out. Feel free to spend your breaks here if you like, but I tend to stay in the office for the night shifts."

Allen stepped in and bumped into the coat rack, backed up a step, and hit the table with the back of his knees. "Why's that?"

"It's bigger and there's a chair. May as well hang out there when the manager isn't working." Don slapped him on the back.

Allen hung up his coat and signed in before they continued.

"Now, this hallway sucks." Don waved his arm out like a master of ceremonies introducing some foreign wonder to an audience. "It leads to the rest of the manor though, so you can't avoid it."

"Um, why?" Allen peered down the short hallway, trying to find something wrong with it. Don's exuberant tour and quirky manner were grating on him. It was like Don wanted him to be scared of the place. He shuffled from one foot to the other, doing his best to sound interested.

"Because the only other way is back out and through the

25

front door. I'm not sure you're ready for the front door, and who wants to go outside in the winter?"

"No. Why does it suck?"

"Got a watch?" Don waggled an eyebrow.

"I use my phone." Allen took the device out of his pocket.

"Great, make it be a stopwatch." Don whistled, waiting.

Allen flipped through several screens, finding the function.

"Did they tell you about the time thing in the interview?"

Allen shook his head while he brought up the stopwatch.

"It's crazy, but it isn't consistent in the building. That is, there are some places where time's messed up, but it's always the same—the time being weird, I mean."

Allen looked up from his phone, eyes narrow.

"How long do you think it should take us to get down this hallway?" Don smiled and swayed with frantic energy.

"Probably ten seconds." Allen tilted his head to the side. "Can't be more than a few metres." He smirked when Don faced the other way.

"Start the clock!" Don's smile widened as he waved his hands around again.

Allen did and Don led him down the hallway, walking backwards.

"Now, everything seems fine to us." Don stared at him.

Allen nodded.

When they reached the end of the short walk, Don put out his hands. "Check your phone."

Allen almost dropped it when he noticed nearly three minutes had been recorded.

"You can try it again if you'd like." Don winked. "We've got the time."

Allen went to the hostess room and back. Both treks resulted in a recorded time much longer than the walk should have taken. He put a hand on Don's shoulder and gaped at his phone.

"There are all sorts of those things around here. Don't worry, most of it is harmless."

"It's unbelievable. How does it do that?" Allen checked the settings on his phone. "Does everyone know about that?"

Don rocked on his heels. "Everyone who works here."

Allen froze. "We have to tell people. It's amazing!"

"Most people won't believe you. The ones who do, no one will believe them. There was a news story about it back before I started here. It was pretty much a fluff piece. Other than a few weirdoes who came to check it out, no one cares."

"But it changes everything we know about—everything." He stared down the hallway, mouth open.

Don patted his shoulder. "You can go ahead with that, but I'm telling you, it won't make a difference. We had a ghost hunter here a few years back. Did a whole study on the entire manor."

"What happened?"

"Disappeared." Don shrugged. "The great hall's this way." He continued around another corner leaving Allen at the brink of the anomaly.

He blinked rapidly at it, struggling to understand what was going on in the hallway.

"It'll still be there later," Don called back.

Allen hurried to the large entrance hall. A couch and some armchairs were arranged around a large concrete fireplace. A chandelier hung low. At its base was a large brass ball, and from the middle, spindly arms reached up, topped with pointed bulbs. It looked like a huge metal spider and Allen made sure to not walk under it. Paintings and tapestries hung on the walls and a wide, grand staircase twisted up to the second floor. Everything from the fixtures to the furniture was in questionable, well-used condition. Closed doors on either side of the room hinted at more aged opulence beyond.

"This is where you would have ended up if you'd have made it through the front door." Don pointed to a broad wooden entryway and an equally large inner door, not as faded as its twin, but cracked down the middle. "There's a little foyer between the big doors. One side is a coatroom and the other is a secret door."

Allen's eyes went wide. "Secret door? Now you're talking." He set his dilemma over the time-bending hallway aside and hurried over to the wall, searching for a sconce to pull or a subtle switch to press.

Don cleared his throat. "It's not like this is Webster. It is a dead end now. Leads to the men's room. It used to just go through to the other side, nothing exciting."

Allen deflated with a long breath. He left the lost secret and went back to the middle of the room. He caught the smirk Don gave him and thought he seemed happy to disappoint.

Don walked to the large inner door and stopped at a dresser set up to one side. He opened the drawer, showing the loose papers inside. "We keep sign-in junk here. Just let the guests take the sheets over near the fireplace to fill them out on the coffee table. Most people have already paid, so they just have to sign the forms. If we get any unexpected guests, we have to take them to the office and book their rooms on the computer.

"The manager puts the room keys and pamphlets and stuff in here the day of the booking. Just greet them and hand them the package." Don closed the drawer with a slam. "Make sure they sign though—right away."

"Why?" Allen moved closer.

"Legal stuff." Don spun away from the dresser and pointed at the huge staircase. "Try to use these stairs as often as you can. They're the quick ones. It's a pain coming out here just to get upstairs, but it works."

Allen stepped back. "They look safer."

"Yeah, that too."

"Is there any time thing in this room?" Allen scanned the place, imagining the horrible things going on around him, hiding outside his perception.

"See those glass doors on either side of the fireplace?" Don pointed to them. He put a hand on Allen's shoulder standing close.

"Yeah." The word came out as a squeak. Allen cleared his throat and wiped his clammy hands on his pants. He shuffled a step away.

"They lead to the back patio and garden. We put a statue in front of the door on the right. Use the left."

A low, wide statue of a kid riding a lion blocked the narrow door.

"What happens if you go out that way?"

Don shrugged. "Not sure. Caretaker told me about that one. I just avoid it." He let go of Allen and scratched his cheek.

Allen took in the hollow state of the room and tried to incorporate the strange concepts casually explained to him. "What? Why?"

"I just figured it was bad news and should steer clear. Why risk it?" Don nudged him.

Allen took a minute to work out the possibilities, his face contorting as he worked through the confusion and fear he felt. "Is that all?"

"The door on the wall to the left leads to a sitting room." Don walked over and opened it. "This used to be a lady's drawing room. Some guests really want to go in there. I try to dissuade them, but I relent if they push it. No need to get anyone upset, right?"

"What's happens in there?" Allen took a deep breath to prepare for the answer. He stood in the doorway next to Don and shivers ran wild up and down his spine.

"See those big mirrors in there—that's another thing."

Don stopped abruptly and spun around to face Allen, causing him to jump.

"Don't look directly at any of the mirrors in the building. It's not dangerous, but you'll see something then end up stuck staring at it. These are the biggest mirrors in the place and seem to be the most potent."

Allen's eyes widened and he tightened his mouth, forming a frown. "What do you see?"

"Me, personally? I see a girl I knew in high school. It's different for everyone. I was stuck there for an entire night once. The manager had to come and find me in the morning. Just keep it in mind okay? Glancing is fine, just-don't-stare." Don shook his finger as if scolding a child.

"Yeah, I think." Allen's hands trembled. He made fists to steady them.

"And if you do let someone in there, make sure to check on them every hour or so. They almost all get caught, but don't tell them. Just get their attention and let them think they were daydreaming."

"Why can't you tell them?" Allen stole a peek at the long mirror over the drawing room fireplace, met his own eyes, and looked away.

"You can. It's just easier to let it slide. We don't want to freak out our guests, do we?" He nudged Allen and patted his back with a smile.

Allen returned his big smile, but it quickly faded into a grimace.

"There is a dining room on this side too. You can get to it through the drawing room." He pointed at a set of French doors in the room. "Or the door off the slow hallway." He indicated with his thumb over his shoulder then went over to it.

Allen followed a step behind him, tiptoeing.

"We serve breakfast and dinner in there. Nothing weird as far as I've seen. The caretaker says she saw a ghost in there once, but I think she's getting a bit paranoid from living here."

Allen peeked in, but stopped before crossing the threshold.

Don pointed across the great hall. "That door leads to the library and what was the men's lounge and billiard room. Time gets weird in there again. It's slow, so if you're inside, it seems to go by way too quickly. The guests tend to think it's just one of those time flies things. I like to put them in there when I have to do paperwork or cleaning or whatever. Serve some drinks and come back in a couple hours, seems like it's only been half that to them." Don led the way over and held the door open.

Allen slinked to the edge of the room and peered in. To one side he saw the book-lined wall, plush leather chairs, and a large desk at the window. An antique globe stood in a corner. The door blocked the view to the other side, but the bookshelves continued, suggesting more of the same. He imagined someone like Laurier or Mackenzie would have a room like that—a study. He was tempted to go take a closer look, but the fear of the time distortion kept him in the doorway.

"That's the great hall." Don opened his hands wide. "For the most part, you can avoid any trouble spots except the hallway to the office. I find it a pretty nice place to be. Want to go poke around upstairs?"

Allen followed him towards the stairs. The door swung shut behind them with a loud clack making him jump. "When are the guests coming?"

The question stopped Don on the first step of the grand staircase.

"Not for a couple hours still. We have lots of time." He winked again and motioned for Allen to catch up.

Allen swallowed hard and balled up his hands.

The wide, deep stairs were covered in a plush, Oriental carpet. Each step creaked and groaned like a symphony of age as he climbed. Halfway up, they reached a landing with a table and a couple of chairs. Even with the furniture, there was plenty of room to get by. Allen imagined people sitting there and wondered what they would be doing.

At the top, a hallway led off left and right.

Don stood in the middle of the junction and Allen stopped at the top step.

"Other than the caretaker's apartment over the office, it's pretty much just guest rooms up here." Don indicated the direction of the apartment with a nod. "There are eight rooms but we only rent out six of them. Ronnie is in the first room." Don pointed down the left hallway. "We keep room two vacant."

Allen followed Don's actions, but he was distracted by his trembling hands.

Don continued, clapping his hands in an exaggerated gesture. "Rooms three and four are there too. Down the other way are five through eight. I put tonight's bookings in five and six, across the hall from each other. I like to leave eight free when we can. Gives a buffer for the apartment."

"What should I avoid?" Allen felt sweat collect on his brow. A bead ran down his back. He thought about the strange and dangerous phenomenon on the main floor and was alert for signs of it upstairs.

"Room two, obviously. Never go in there. I did on a bet once, didn't sleep for a week. I don't like to even go passed it." Don took a step in the room's direction. "You'll have to, to get to Ronnie's room. He gets his meals in there sometimes. I try to check on him once a day. He's a bit bonkers and makes a bunch of noise from time to time, but nice enough."

Allen peeked around the banister and wiped the sweat

from his forehead. He couldn't believe Don's calm manner, talking about rooms that gave him nightmares.

"Other than that, it's just the back stairs again and the hall closet. I think it's the strangest place after room two." Don looked over his shoulder and smiled.

Allen glanced down each side of the hallway, as if the closet were able to appear anywhere. "Where's that?" His teeth chattered.

"All the way at the end." Don pointed past the first set of rooms. "Just avoid that whole area if you can. I tried to get it blocked off, but here we are." He shrugged.

Allen took a deep breath and clenched his fists. "What's in room two?" The words came out fast and jumbled.

"I don't really know. Whatever it is, it's got to be the cause of all the creepy stuff in here."

"And the closet?" Allen took a step back and stood stiffly against whatever malevolent force was down the hallway.

"Remember that ghost hunter I mentioned?"

Allen nodded.

"He went in there following some reading on his instruments. Haven't seen him since. After the first few hours, I checked on him, but when I opened the door, he wasn't there."

"Maybe he just left?"

"I checked around. Whether it's the closet or not, he disappeared. I get brave enough to check in the closet every few months or so but it's not easy to go down there." Don snapped his fingers and sauntered back.

"Did you go in?" Allen grabbed at Don's shirt.

"Hell no." He moved Allen's hands away. "I haven't put more than a toe in there. It's freaky. It's all cold and eats up any light you shine in it." He shook in an exaggerated shiver.

"How can you stand this place?" Allen's voice creaked.

"It's scary sometimes, but it's a good job. Kinda neat, actually, if you don't let it get to you." Don looked around the old manor.

"I don't think I can do it." Allen backed down the stairs a few steps.

"What, the job? It's not all that bad. Think about it. Working here makes us special. In a weird way, sure, but we get to be part of this place." He put his hand on the railing and smiled. "Special."

"You're teasing me." Allen squirmed away and pointed at Don. He felt a wide, hollow smile creep across his face. "This is all some kind of initiation. I don't even believe in ghosts."

"The caretaker is the one who says there are ghosts. I don't believe in them either. As far as initiations, no need in a place like this." Don winked.

"If it isn't ghosts, what is it?"

"Physics?"

"What does that mean?"

"I don't know. I'm no scientist. I just figure it's got to be some kind of space-time thing." Don spread his hands. "All I can tell you is, I've worked here for years and I'm fine. There's nothing to worry about. Except room two and that closet. Seriously, don't go down there."

A loud bang made Allen jump. "That came from room two." He slipped on a step and grabbed the railing to stop from falling.

"Naw, it's probably Ronnie moving the furniture around."

The sound of cracking wood filled the hallway again. Allen froze but Don walked over to room one and banged on the door. "Ronnie, you okay in there?"

Allen yelped at a third bang and backed farther down the stairs. "That was from room two! It's coming from room two!"

34

"I told you, there's nothing in there."

The door to room two burst open. Don jumped and Allen tripped down the stairs, screaming. A man with a long knotted beard, torn clothes, and wide, bloodshot eyes slammed the door behind him.

"Hey, the ghost hunter! I was just talking about you."

Uninvited Guest

Uninvited Guest
Ben Van Dongen

The cube sat in the middle of the living room and took up space like a toddler demanding attention. Don took a step towards it.

"Don't." Kim grabbed Don's arm and pulled him away from the object now residing in her apartment. "Don't touch it."

Don stopped and scratched his chin. "You said it just appeared?"

"I went to the kitchen to grab my phone charger, and when I came back, it was here. I don't even know where my coffee table went."

The thing was four feet on every side, and looked like it was made of orange metallic Jell-O. Light from the overhead fixture and a nearby lamp reflected off the shiny surface. It seemed to undulate as Don walked around it.

He leaned in, wanting to see if it was slimy or it just appeared that way—like frogs sometimes do. "What does it do?"

"I don't know. It just sits there being creepy." Kim crossed her arms and scrunched up her eyebrows at it, keeping her distance from the intruder.

"And you called me over?"

"You have more experience with weird things than anyone else I could think of. You're forever going on about the stuff that happens when you're working at that hotel." She bit her lip and threw her hands in the air. "I don't know what to do, Don."

"Does anyone else know about it?" He took another step back to keep from reaching out to touch it.

"Beth knows. She was supposed to be coming over. I thought I should warn her."

"She's still coming?" Don kept his focus on the object. Beth often pestered him about the oddities in the hotel but he didn't think she would want to experience something for herself. Kicking his shoes off, he stepped onto the couch and peered at the top of the object.

"She seemed pretty excited about it, so yeah?"

Don tilted his head. "Have you tried to talk to it?"

"And what? Offer it a cup of tea?" Kim exhaled sharply. She grimaced at Don, a hand on her hip.

Don shrugged and raised an eyebrow. He got off the couch and put his shoes back on.

"No." She rolled her eyes. "I haven't talked to it."

"Hello." Don waved to the cube. "Do you want a cup of tea?" He smiled back at Kim, hoping to get an annoyed expression out of her.

"Nothing is coming." The statement emanated from the thing in a voice he thought suited an insurance broker, not a possibly gelatinous cube. Kim covered her mouth and Don backed away then leaned closer.

"I didn't expect that." Don put an arm around her.

"What do you suppose it means?" She shrugged his arm

off and stepped back.

"Hopefully, what it said. Nothing is coming. It sounds fairly benign." Don scratched his cheek.

The front door slammed open causing both Don and Kim to jump. Beth came bursting into the apartment, eyes wide. She saw the cube and clambered over the couch to get to it. She took off her coat, and threw it towards the coat hanger mounted on the wall without breaking eye contact with the thing.

"What did I miss?"

"It just spoke." Kim put a hand on her brow and sighed.

"It said nothing is coming." Don eyed Beth, standing between her and the object.

"Hi, Don. What did it say?" She pushed him to the side with one hand.

Kim hung up the discarded coat. "It said, 'Nothing is coming'."

"That's ominous as hell." Beth beamed at the others before going back to eyeing the object.

"You think so?" Don moved next to her in front of the cube, viewing the object from her lower angle. "I got that feeling, but it sounded genuine."

Kim humphed and sighed loudly, rolling her eyes as she headed to the kitchen.

Beth moved around the cube, inspecting it. "What the heck does genuine mean?"

Don followed her. "It means forthcoming, frank, honest."

"I mean, how can this thing be genuine?"

He shrugged. "I guess you have to hear it."

"You thinking alien?" Beth got low to the carpeted floor and crawled around the cube on her hands and knees.

"Could be anything, really. Maybe it's an experiment."

Beth snapped up straight. "Or a test!"

"It'd be a pretty lame test."

"Strange what it said. Did it just blurt it out?"

Don straightened and stretched his back. "No. I asked it if it wanted tea."

She cocked an eyebrow at him.

He shrugged.

"It's like Odysseus and the Cyclops isn't it?"

"How so?" Don glanced at the kitchen as he sat on the couch.

"When Odysseus poked out the Cyclops' eye, it demanded to know who he was. He said his name was Nobody."

"Uh huh." Don crossed his legs and leaned back, stifling a yawn.

"Well, whenever anyone asked who poked out his eye, all he could tell them was that Nobody did it. They must have thought he was dense, even for a Cyclops. Poor guy couldn't even get revenge."

"So you think Nothing could be the name of a thing?"

"Or a person," Beth frowned at Don over her shoulder. "Maybe." She sat cross-legged on the carpet, close to the shimmering cube.

"Reminds me of the Never-Ending Story."

Kim returned carrying a teapot and cups on a tray. "I'm glad you two are so fascinated, but can we get back to why it's in my living room?" She set it down and joined Don on the couch.

He poured himself a cup and one for Beth, and nodded to Kim.

Beth reached over and took the cup. She jolted upright, sending the tea in her mug sloshing over the rim, and turned to Don. "Hey, ever see anything like this at the Manor?"

"Now that you mention it, something exactly like this doesn't happen every other month, no."

Beth smacked his arm, causing him to spill some of his

own drink.

He put the cup down and shook the hot tea off his hand, sneering at her. "Thanks."

Kim grimaced and went to the kitchen. She came back with a dishrag and cleaned the spill, exhaling sharply as she soaked it up. When she was done, she refilled Don's cup and dropped the wet rag on the tray.

"We could try asking it something else." Don wiped his pants as the tea seeped into the denim.

"Why are you here?" Beth asked the cube.

"Nothing is coming," it said again, in the same tone.

"Wow." Beth blinked and her mouth hung open.

"The voice?" Don smirked.

Beth got up. "Yeah, not what I expected."

Kim stirred sugar into her tea. "Where did it come from?"

"What? From the cube." Beth shook her head at Kim.

"But where? It doesn't have a mouth."

Don picked up his drink and glanced from Beth to Kim. "It's almost like I heard it in my ear. Does that sound right?"

Beth dropped back onto the couch. "Well, we definitely heard it. Like a sound." She peered into her cup then drank what was left in it.

They sat quietly and drank their tea, watching the cube.

Kim folded her hands in her lap. "I don't like it."

Don turned in his seat to face her. "I don't think there is anything to be worried about."

"No? I shouldn't be worried about this thing that appeared in my living room replacing my coffee table? This weird, creepy box thing that speaks and we have no idea what it is or where it came from? It's just fine?"

Don put a hand on Kim's arm. "That's not what I mean. I'm just saying, nothing bad has happened. It could be no big deal. This sort of thing happens at the manor—"

"It's not in your house!"

Don scrunched his nose. "Sorry." He blinked and smiled, wide-eyed. "But is it your house?"

Beth leaned closer. "What are you getting at?"

"What if this is just a replica of Kim's house—or this could have been the thing's house all along and we're the invaders?"

"Like it had a home here or it lived in this apartment?"

"Stop it!" Kim clenched the hem of her skirt. "You two are starting to get under my skin. This thing showing up in my apartment is creepy enough without you coming up with these theories."

"Come on, Kim, this is amazing," Beth said. "Has anyone ever heard of anything like this before?"

"Maybe it happens all the time but no one is ever left to tell anyone about it." Kim held her arms tightly against herself.

Don stood and eyed the dimensions of the room. "We could try to move it."

Kim grabbed his arm. "Don't. Please." She pulled him back onto the couch.

"I'll ask it." Beth smiled. "Hey, cube thing, are you dangerous? Can we move you?"

"Nothing is coming," it said in its calm, professional voice.

"What is nothing?" Don asked.

"Nothing is coming."

"Don's probably right, Kim. This thing is strange, but we've been here with it, and we're all right. It's probably fine—inconvenient, but no big deal." Beth tipped her cup back then looked into it, squinting.

Kim picked up her cup, staring ahead, face tightly set. She went to take a sip but put the cup down with a loud clank. "Shouldn't we at least call someone?" She stood and took a few steps away from the cube.

"Who?" Beth asked. "The police?"

Don shifted to look over the back of the couch at Kim. "What about the university?"

Beth took hold of her empty cup, waving it with a flourish as she spoke. "Whatever you do, you don't want to get the government involved."

"If anyone believes you, it'll probably just be some kook and no one's gonna believe them." Don scratched his cheek.

"Why does it have to be my living room?" Kim exhaled and covered her face. "Nothing like this ever happens to anyone else I know."

"I think you're looking at this the wrong way." Don poured Beth and himself a second cup of tea. He held up Kim's cup, but she ignored him so he left it mostly empty. "It could be some blessing, or gift. What if it's a prize of some kind? Have you entered any secret competitions lately?" Don laughed. Beth smacked his leg and he stopped.

Beth shrugged. "It could be a good thing."

"How is a creepy alien cube, sitting in my apartment, a good thing?"

Don wagged a finger at Kim. "We don't know that it's alien."

"It could be," Beth added.

"It could be a modern art piece—I still don't want it in my living room."

Don chuckled. "What if it's like a magic lamp?"

"Stop trying to touch it, you weirdo." Kim smacked him on the shoulder.

Beth hit him on the other side. "Let him."

"I don't want to have to explain to the cops that my idiot friend was vaporized after touching the weird scary box."

"Nothing is here," the cube said.

Don froze, halfway out of his seat.

"What?" Beth glanced from Don to the cube and back—her face sunk.

"It said, 'Nothing is here'." Don peered down at it.

Kim backed away until she was against the wall. She reached back and felt for the doorway to the kitchen.

"What did you say?" Beth asked the cube. She stood rigid. It didn't answer. "What did it say?"

Don went to the window and searched the street. "Check the hallway." He left the window and saw Beth with her eye to the peephole, moving back and forth, scanning the hall through the distorted view.

"Anything there?" Don ran over.

"Hallway's empty. The street?"

"No, nothing strange." He looked over at the cube and smiled.

Beth scrunched her face. "What?"

"Nothing." He chuckled. "Nothing is here." He nudged her.

Beth snorted and Don doubled over with laughter.

"Nothing," he managed to say between the fits. "Kim, did you hear that? Kim?"

As Big As Love

As Big As Love
Christian Laforet

I lean in and inhale. She smells like twilight after the rain…like summer days long past…like heaven. I have never loved until this moment. I am nearly lost in the enormity of it, like a toddler playing with the concept of God. I have not even begun to fully understand what the word means before now…

**

Inside the pod, a light begins to flash. A series of very specific bursts of illumination initiates a cascade of synaptic nerves firing. Neurotransmitters carry complex signals to the brain. Within moments, the man in the pod stirs.

His sleep has been the thing of fables. A mythological achievement usually reserved for gods, trolls, dragons, and great beauties. During his slumber, religions, empires, and races have all risen and fallen.

The faintest hint of life, an eye fluttering open, sends a tiny whirl of air sweeping through the pod. It is the first significant action to take place in over a million years.

The strobe is now accompanied by a melodious chime. A soft series of tones issues from speakers embedded in the pod on either side of his head. The sounds float like ghosts down forgotten hallways to his brain. Electrons spark across grey matter. Feelings, emotions...memories, dance through his mind.

The cycle runs through to completion. With a snap, followed by an extensive hiss, the pod's compression seal breaks and slowly, mechanically, the top hatch lifts.

His thoughts swirl inside his head like a vortex.

He is age three, and it is Christmas morning. A shiny red tricycle awaits him underneath the tree.

He is fourteen and starting his first day of high school. He is not prepared for the experience and wants to run home.

He is seventeen and he has lost his virginity. He thinks he is in love. He is wrong.

He is nineteen and he works in the kitchen at a family restaurant. He hates the job but hates school more.

He is twenty-five and he stands solemnly at his parents' funeral. Their deaths are so unexpected he has not been able to fully absorb them.

He is thirty-six and works at a factory. The money is good, but the hours are terrible.

He is forty and he sees her for the first time. She takes his breath away.

He is forty-two and they have been together for almost a year. He has never been happier. He has found true love.

He is forty-four and he sits outside a doctor's office, worrying about her. He wrings his hat between his hands as he waits for something, anything, to take him away from there.

He is forty-six and the last year has been as close to hell as he has ever suffered. The days are filled with medication and monitoring.

He is forty-seven and the world around him has lost all meaning. The sun can no longer warm him. She is gone...forever.

He is forty-eight and he has a vision.

He is forty-nine and he begins work on the ship.

He is fifty-six and he is almost finished.

He is fifty-seven and with a final breath of relief, he activates the autopilot and lies down to sleep in the pod.

He is sixty-one and he is sleeping.

He is a hundred and forty-nine and he is sleeping.

He is fourteen hundred and six and he is sleeping.

He is two hundred thousand, four hundred and ninety-one and he is sleeping.

He is eight hundred thousand and seventeen and he is sleeping.

He is one million, fifty-eight thousand and two and he is sleeping.

Now, he is awake.

With bones older than some stars, he moves.

The memories continue their unflinching montage. He does not want to remember any longer; he can't bear it.

***

I let her pull me in. She is the Garden of Eden and I am Adam. I feel God's light on me as I enjoy the finest fruit the universe has ever known. I am lost in the pleasure. Around me, the world melts away until it is only the two of us. We dance our way into perfect symmetry.

***

He climbs from the pod. His body creaks, mumbling like a forgotten prayer, unpractised like neglected faith. Aches and pains have their way with his old frame.

The ship is designed to do one thing and one thing only—transport a sleeping passenger. Because of this, there is nothing more to the spacecraft than a room big enough for the pod and a view port to look out of. Indeed, even being awake is using up the very small amount of oxygen inside the cabin. He isn't worried, though. As he stumbles towards the viewport, he can see the ship's programming has functioned just as intended. He is right where he wants to be.

The planet before him is immense.

Touchdown is surprisingly gentle.

The hatch to the shuttle opens smoothly considering the unimaginable distance and time it has traversed.

The spacesuit, which has been carbon packed in a small cube along the wall opposite his sleep pod, fits him perfectly. It feels like he sealed the suit in the cube yesterday. Then again, to him, it has only been a single day. Over three hundred and sixty-five million nights all in one.

The scene before him is exactly what he had seen in his vision. Lights dance as nature and technology meld together. The city extends out like the tides. It is majestic and awe-inspiring. He does not take in the view for long before he climbs from the ship, now powering down for the last time. With a grunt, he begins walking towards the spires of glass, technology, air, and circuits.

***

Our time together stretches into infinity but it is not enough. Even infinity is as short as the blink of an eye when compared to the vastness of love.

With a final explosion, which causes the stars to move and the heavens to shake, we finish.

We are thrust back into the reality we started in, back into a bed in a house on a street in a city in a country on a world in the universe. We are small again, but it doesn't matter because, for a moment, we were gods. For a brief instant, we sat atop the galaxy and nothing else mattered, everything in existence was beneath our notice. With panting breath and sweaty skin, we lie. I know I have never felt love like this before. I commit all to this woman. She is my core...my sun. She is everything that ever was and ever will be. I will do anything for her...

***

The grass beneath his feet is soft. Each step is a pleasure.

As the city grows before him, he can't help but think of his journey. After her departure from his life, he was wracked with a sadness so profound, his soul could not escape its pull. His spirit teetered on the edge of an event horizon which threatened to damn him forever. Deliverance came in the form of the vision. He saw this place—the home of the creators. He envisioned how to construct the ship. Now, after eons, he is ready to ask them, where is she? Where do our souls go when we die? Surely, they who gave us thought and will and compassion and...love—surely they have to know.

So he will walk boldly into their city of perfection. He will demand they tell him where to find her, and then he will go there. Even if he has to build another ship and fly to another universe, even if he has to sleep for a million more years, a billion more, he will do it. Because he knows no amount of time, no area of space, is as big as love.

Dead Planet

Dead Planet
Ben Van Dongen

The shuttle sat, connected to the dock, enduring the new decontamination procedures. Three hours in, the quarantine was only half done. The small ship was cramped for the two passengers, and waiting made it feel like it was shrinking. Oswald leaned back in his pilot's chair with his eyes closed. He heard his passenger shift and rustle and knew, from experience, she was frustrated.

"You may as well try to relax."

Lea grumbled loudly. "It's a waste of time." The sound of a tapping foot highlighted her mood.

He had heard it all. As her personal pilot for the last year and a bit, he could recount her rant before she uttered it. It boiled down to the resented waste of time and forced confinement. She would recite the statistics—how tens of thousands of transports flew from Earth to the Moon base without incident, and would mention specifically it was unlikely the private ship of a brilliant scientist would be the first to break the streak.

He interrupted her before she could start. "The decontamination is in place for a reason. You know more about the loss of the Mars Colony than probably anyone. Precaution is prevention." Every schoolchild knew the motto.

"If I didn't have to spend half my time trapped in my own shuttle, I might actually have the answer to what happened to Mars by now." Lea shifted in her seat, pulling at the straps.

"Nothing you can do." Oswald stifled a yawn, attempting to hide it and avoid a lecture. "The space-resistant organisms are spreading. I, personally, am happy that we lean on caution. The last parasite to get through devastated—"

"I know!" Lea hit the console.

"Hey!" Oswald sat up in his seat and glared at her. He shook his head before settling back down.

"If I could spend my time doing my work, if they would let me go to Mars, I could find a solution. How many times do I have to explain it to you?"

"I'm not the one you have to convince."

"Do you disagree?"

"Are you saying you're above the protocols?" Oswald stretched, feeling a sigh from Lea on the back of his hand.

She grumbled and knocked it away. "I have traveled between the Earth, the Moon, and the asteroid mines more than anyone else on record."

"Then you should know. Everyone has to go through it. It's the only defense we have."

"What if there's an emergency?" Lea rehashed the points she made during every quarantine.

"We could handle it in ship."

"What if this were a merchant ship?"

"Thankfully, this isn't."

"But what if?"

"Then men in white suits would take care of it. Every situation has a HAZMAT contingency." Oswald opened his eyes and smiled at Lea.

"Waste of time. People could die by the time they suit up. Besides, you've seen them. You can't tell me you'd trust your life to those bozos."

"No, but I've got you to save me." He patted her leg and she swatted his hand away again.

"This is serious."

"I know. I'm being serious. I'm with the number one biologist, skilled archaeologist, geologist, and a pretty good MD. I'm the safest person in the world right here." He shut his eyes again.

"We're not on Earth. We're cramped in a tiny ship, sitting at a damn airlock!"

Oswald shrugged his shoulders.

"Airlock now pressurizing. Thank you for your patience." The automated announcement was broadcasted over their comm.

Oswald sat up to his controls, flicking switches, putting the ship to sleep. "Hey—they shaved off five minutes."

"Joy." Lea unstrapped her antigravity equipment locker, which floated, ready to be guided, and the bag containing hazardous samples.

Oswald grabbed his own small bag and a few more of Lea's and followed her through the passageway and onto Moon Base VII.

The corridors were narrow and low. Lea fit fine, but Oswald kept his head down and ducked into rooms. The hallway off of the docking facility opened into a large dome with heavily tinted and shielded transparent panels. There was a registration desk and the security station in the wide-open space. The earlier moon bases were larger and more elegant, but the new ones were sparse and utilitarian, designed for scientists, not diplomats. A large rock jutting up from the surface was left bare in the center of the room, roped off like a statue. The whole structure used gravitomagnetic superconductors to produce gravity, but even at the massive scale, true Earth gravity wasn't possible, resulting in things being lighter. Walking in the base took getting used to; even the experienced staff looked like marionettes striding down the halls.

Several more tubes led off to small domes separated into living quarters, the lab, a dining hall, and recreation areas. At every junction a double set of open hatches could be sealed in case of a leak or contamination risk. Signs pointed the way to each area, but a security guard greeted Lea and directed her anyway.

"I know where I'm going." Lea waved her hand to dismiss him and his help. She walked past without making eye contact.

Oswald smiled at the jilted man. He shrugged under the bags he carried and let the guard take a few from him. "Thanks."

Lea, her expression severe, headed for the lab with her equipment and samples floating in front of her. Oswald went with security to the living quarters and dumped the luggage. The walls of the dome curved down sharply and the bunks were in rows across the open floor, the ones near the walls lacking headroom. He shook the guard's hand and flopped on the nearest bed, a standard issue with military lumps and a scratchy blanket, to take a nap.

***

The dome for the lab was small and set at the end of a long corridor. A solid workbench curved around the outer wall, pushed back to leave headroom. Stations were set up along the bench with identical sets of equipment. Complicated and expensive machines in the center could accommodate several people working on individual projects with limited, but necessary, interaction.

A dozen scientists in white coats worked fluidly, criss-crossing in a seamless pattern. Lea burst in and bullied her way onto a whole lab station for herself. She didn't bother telling the lesser scientists who she was—they would already know.

She opened her case and readied the equipment to analyze the samples from the Martian impact. She smiled at the tiny rocks. The process of getting the minute samples off Mars took ingenuity. It was her idea to deliberately send an asteroid to the restricted planet and collect the ejected fragments for study, but they had to be decontaminated first. She wasn't even allowed to collect them herself. Even in a secure lab on the moon, fear of what killed the Mars colony caused panic. Her smile faded as she set the case in the machine. "Terrified idiots."

It had taken her two frustrating years of committee meetings, government inquiry, and arguments to get the mission approved. Threats, legal action, and publicity finally swayed the ruling in her direction. Being a top scientist and public figure helped. She would have preferred to work on the Martian debris in her own lab on Earth, but that was another battle she'd lost.

The samples, stored in sealed, protected containers, were only accessible once the lengthy scan and decontamination process had determined no deadly pathogen or parasite had survived.

Lea placed the clear boxes into the slot of the scanner and closed the lid, fastening it. The machine automatically set to work running the tests.

She tapped a closely trimmed nail against her teeth as the process cleansed the samples of the clues she searched for. As the process neared completion, she breathed out a quiet whistle of forced air. She had argued to the council that the point of the mission was to determine what had been transferred to Mars and wiped out the colony. The fear of contamination was too much for the powers that be to overcome, and she had to be satisfied with an initial, small victory.

A chime rang out, notifying Lea the samples were ready for testing. She opened the case and at the sight of the rust-coloured rocks, the other scientists fled. The last one slammed the emergency hatch closed, running towards the decontamination chambers.

"Amateurs." Lea set to work. "No—idiots."

***

A vigorous shaking woke Oswald. He snorted and sat up with a jolt seeing the security guard standing over him.

"Sorry to bother you." The man wrung his hands, his face pale. "There's been an incident in the lab."

Oswald shot out of bed and ran past the guard. He ducked into the connector tube and sprinted to the main dome, skidding as he changed directions, heading for the lab. Another security officer stopped him at the tunnel junction.

"You can't go down there. We have a contamination risk." The woman was smaller than Oswald, but her stance made him stop. The other guard trotted up behind him.

"Where is she?" He breathed heavily.

The woman looked back down the tube. "Still in the lab. Your doctor trashed it."

"So go get her." He gestured past her.

"We've had to put the facility on lockdown. We're probably all contaminated already. She has Martian samples." She whispered the last words.

"I'll risk it. Let me go get her." Oswald rolled his eyes. He was almost as tired of the taboo and rampant fear as Lea was.

"She's probably infected with something. She's crazed. If you go down there, you're on your own."

68

"It's just a temper tantrum." He covered his mouth and yawned. "I'll settle her down."

Confidently, and amused at the awed looks he was given, Oswald ducked into the corridor and walked to the lab.

The guard yelled after him. "We're sealing you in!"

***

"Lea?" The door was closed, so he peeked through the small window set into it and something smashed against it, making him jump. He pressed the door release and hugged the outer wall.

"Lea? It's just me. You're freaking out the nice guards. They woke me up."

She screamed and threw another beaker.

Oswald thought it may have been a graduated cylinder as it flew past him and hit the corridor wall, but he wasn't sure. "What the heck is going on?" He moved into the open doorway and crouched, waiting to duck out of the way of any other flying apparatus.

"Decontamination!" Her yell was guttural and venomous. "I'm so close and those paranoid fart monkeys keep holding me back with their protocols!" She smashed another something breakable on the floor and stomped on it, slipping.

Oswald rushed over and caught her arm. "I just want to point out that you said fart monkeys, but I don't want you to throw anything at me."

Lea slumped and rubbed her eyes. Oswald's grip on her arm kept her from falling.

"There's broken glass down there you know." It looked like every piece of equipment had been damaged by Lea's furious conniption. He couldn't name them all, but the destruction was evident.

"Shut up." Lea straightened and shook off his grasp. "I'm so close." She clenched her fists.

Used to her temper and outbursts, he gave her some leeway. He attributed her childish behaviour to being so smart and living a strange life. She had told him she'd graduated university at nine, or something. She was used to getting what she wanted, especially in the scientific community. He had only seen her cry once, though, and she appeared very close to doing it again.

"It's all right." He focused his gaze on her and tried to sound comforting and not anxious. "Like you said, it's a step in the right direction."

"It's not good enough." Lea fought for composure and shuddered as she breathed. "I thought I could use the dead matter to examine the cause of the outbreak, but the new procedure scrubbed the rocks clean. There's nothing here, not even carcasses or imprints."

He put an arm around her. "I know it's frustrating, but you knew it was going to take time."

"I can't carry it anymore." She huffed and covered her eyes but tears leaked past her hands, betraying her.

Oswald held her closer. "It's not your responsibility. You've done more to fight for answers than anyone. Without your work, we might have never known it was a pathogen that killed everyone on the colony or even that they're a risk. Remember when people thought it was an alien invasion, or ghosts?"

"Oswald." She pushed him away. Her tone took an edge that punched through the falling tears. "I don't know."

"What?" He smiled, not sure what she meant.

"I don't know if it was a pathogen. I thought it was and I fudged the results. I thought I could prove it later, but everything's been a dead end." She grunted and kicked at the glass on the floor.

Oswald blinked and his mouth dropped open. "What exactly are you saying?"

"I thought it was a pathogen. It probably is, but the tests

I've been able to do show conflicting results. A space-faring pathogen has to be involved, but nothing we've been able to find shows the kind of contagious and deadly infection that can completely kill an entire colony."

Oswald turned away from her. "You lied?" He stared at a tipped apparatus dangling from a power cord. A crack ran along its plastic casing. He rubbed his face and chewed on his lip.

"I was sure. I'd already proved we were transmitting and mutating viruses, bacteria, and microscopic organisms between colonies. It made sense."

"But it could have been something else." Oswald faced her again.

Lea nodded like a scolded child.

"It could have been anything?"

She nodded again.

He headed for the door.

"Where are you going?"

"We have to tell them."

Lea grabbed his arm. "No. We'll never get there if they find out." Her shoes slid in the glass.

"You've been lying for years. Everything we think happened, the largest tragedy in space travel. It set us back decades and we have no idea why?" He turned on her, finger raised, breathing heavily, shaking with anger, but he stopped short.

"Oswald. You have to help me. You know I'm still the best chance we have at figuring it all out."

His initial anger faded. "My dad died on Mars." He looked at the dome's roof and spotted the red planet, a dot of light in the sky. He pictured his father's face.

"I know. If it gets out that it may not have been an infection they'll never let anyone go there. We have to. We have to go to Mars. The satellite images, thermal sensors, probes, nothing we've sent there has given any indication about why over a hundred thousand people died a violent, rapid death. I can." She dug her fingers into his arm. Her tears had stopped as she implored, trying to convince him she was right.

"What can you do? You just told me you were wrong and lied about it." Oswald pulled away from Lea's grip. Her nails left red marks on his arm.

"I can figure it out. I am the smartest person on any planet and I have dedicated my life to solving this. If I can get to Mars, I can see for myself what happened. You can get me there." Lea walked in front of Oswald and met his eyes.

"They'll never let us go, even if they don't find out you lied."

"You have to take me anyway. Drop me off and leave me if you have to. I need to see what's there. I have to see what killed Mars."

Oswald left the lab, punching the doorframe on the way out. His hand bounced off the synthetic material without leaving a mark. He rubbed his sore knuckles as he walked down the corridor, leaving her surrounded by her mess.

***

The door leading to the main dome was sealed. Oswald tapped on the porthole and a masked face appeared.

A speaker crackled overhead. "Step back sir. This area is on lockdown."

"It's fine. There's no outbreak. You can secure the area."

"We have to determine that for ourselves. Step back please."

He did and the door hissed open.

Nearly every guard in the station was on the other side, dressed in HAZMAT gear. Through their masks he saw their eyes track him as they passed. One stepped towards him, but hesitated. They already thought Lea could be infected. He figured they were worried about the same with him.

Another figure in a civilian HAZMAT suit swiped a hand-held scanner over him. When he was cleared to leave the tube, he headed for the shuttle. It was as far away as he could get from the person he had worked with and looked after for the last year. He didn't see anyone else on his way to the docking facility.

Oswald closed the hatch behind him and made sure the audio pickups were disabled then screamed until he was hoarse, wrenching the flight stick violently. He cursed the sturdy construction of the ship then was thankful for it. The cabin was quiet. Oswald rubbed his throat and flicked on the communications and heard half a message from security.

"…appened? Are you contaminated? We have the doctor in lockdown, but we have to know what's causing these violent outbursts. We didn't detect any pathogen in the lab. Your ship is locked in its docking clamps and will not be released until a decontamination of both you and the doctor has—"

"It's fine, take a breath." Oswald closed his eyes and shook his head, frustrated. "There's no problem. We're just not so good at handling disappointment."

"While I can appreciate your candidness, we are going to have to escort you to lockdown for scanning and decontamination. It's not that I don't believe you, it's procedure, sir."

Oswald chuckled. "Yeah, sure. I'm coming out." He smiled, thinking about security taking Lea into custody then burst out laughing when he realized they would be making her endure another full decontamination cycle.

An officer waited to escort him. Even in full gear, she kept her distance. He snickered and snorted his way down the corridors. His behaviour caused people to keep farther back than the guards who'd passed him on his way to the lab, which caused him to laugh harder. People watched him go by, but hid and ducked when he noticed them. He wanted to jump at one of them to see the reaction it would cause, but he assumed they wouldn't get the joke, so he calmly followed the guard to the decontamination chamber.

***

The secure room was even smaller then the ship. It was at the edge of the main dome and the outer wall curved at a drastic angle, cutting down the usable space. Oswald lay on the ground watching the lunar sky through the semi-transparent surface. From the angle, he saw ships zooming to and away from the moon. The entire complex was going through decontamination, but since they were the suspected cause of the phantom outbreak, they were treated with special care.

As he stared at the stars, he waited for Lea to explode with anger. She sat on a bench, holding her hands in her lap, occasionally glancing in his direction. Neither of them spoke. From the time he entered the chamber and saw her fidgeting, he knew she was desperate to talk.

The same automated voice that counted down their time in the ship told them they were entering the final stage of decontamination and had forty-five minutes to go.

"I'm sorry." Lea crossed her arms and sat back, but the curve of the wall pushed her head forward.

"I think that was a record."

"I'm really sorry about everything—the lab, my outbursts, the thing."

"Let it go. I'm still stewing."

"I just—even if you don't help me, or if you tell them what I did. I want you to know that I'm sorry. I mean, I'm sorry to you. And I know I can act like a brat."

Oswald propped himself up on an elbow to face her. "While I appreciate your apology and admitting that you're a brat, I still don't know what I'm going to do. You'll have to keep sitting quietly and let me work it out."

"I—"

Oswald put up a hand then rolled back over. They didn't

speak for the rest of the procedure and, other than Lea's shifting, they didn't move.

When the voice told them they were clear, the door hissed open. The guards stationed outside handed them a tablet with a waiver for them to mark with their thumbprint, clearing the station of the blame.

Oswald walked past with his hands in his pockets. "Stick the boss with the bill. She's the one who wrecked the place."

Lea took the form and marked it. She apologized to the security staff and thanked them.

Oswald's steps wavered when he heard her, but he kept moving forward. He wasn't used to her complying with anything, and she only thanked people sarcastically.

She caught up and followed a step behind. They went to the living quarters to pick up the equipment and bags. Scooping up his bag and the smaller one of hers, he left her to struggle carrying the larger of her own bags and guide the levitating tool locker.

Oswald rolled his head around his neck in a stretch and reminded himself she deserved worse. They walked quietly to the shuttle.

The station occupants openly stared as they passed. Oswald heard a few whispered conversations but didn't bother to listen. He did hear Lea stammer a few times as she started to ask questions, but she managed to stop without him prompting.

They walked through the main dome with the security station and reception. More guards, along with most of the scientists, including the ones Lea had intimidated and frightened, were there under some guise Oswald didn't care about. He saw eager and trepidatious expressions in the group and figured they were there to watch the spectacle of him and Lea being escorted out. They didn't seem to expect Oswald to give them a big smile and a cheery wave or for Lea to stop and apologize to the scientists.

When they were secure in the ship, with the audio pickups still off, Oswald turned to Lea and put a finger up. "Don't."

Her mouth quivered, a question fighting to break free. She choked on the words and cleared her throat.

"We're going to do exactly what I say for this next part." She nodded and sat rigid in her seat.

"I have something to tell you. You are going to sit there and listen while they run the departure scan. At the end, I'm going to ask you a question."

She put her hands in her lap and failed to look relaxed.

"When we were being held, I thought about my father. You know he left for Mars when I was a kid. He was excited to go. It was his dream. I remember him picking me up and spinning me around before he went into the transport.

"I waited for his weekly messages, keeping up with the terraforming in the news. I was proud. I used to brag at school. All my projects had something to do with Mars and the process of making it livable." Oswald faced forward.

"When I was older, I decided I would become a pilot so I could go to Mars myself. I would surprise my dad, and he would show me the work he was doing. I lived for that moment."

Lea reached out and put a hand on Oswald's arm.

"I remember when I heard the Mars Colony was gone. It happened almost overnight. I was looking forward to my weekly talk with Dad, and my mom told me. The worst part was not knowing what happened. Everyone was dead, and there was no clue how or why. I mourned while people around me talked about conspiracies and worried that what happened would somehow make it to Earth." He rubbed his eyes.

"I was sad and angry, and everyone else was scared and paranoid. I decided I would still train to be a pilot. I hoped I would somehow find a way to go there. Maybe I'd go and see my dad was still there, working on something secret or waiting for someone to rescue him." He shifted in his seat to face her, eyebrows scrunched. "When you made the announcement that you'd discovered the pathogen mutation in the colonies and said that's what killed Mars, the whole world let out its breath. They finally had something to blame and something to fight." Oswald looked out the small window.

"Governments and companies worked to solve the pathogen problem. You were famous. You were going to fix the problem on Mars. When I met you on the moon, I had to help anyway I could. I convinced you to make me your pilot because I believed in you. When they denied you access to Mars, I defended you. They had the answer you gave them and were content. I put up with your tantrums and stood up for you and made friends with people who would keep the things you did out of reports. I covered for you, Lea." Oswald rubbed his forehead and wiped away a tear before she could see.

"It's irresponsible for them to close the book on Mars, even if you hadn't lied to them. They are keeping something from everyone. The probe and satellite scans are bullshit. My father deserves better than that." He turned back to her.

"If I can get you to Mars, are you certain you can figure out what happened?"

"Yes." Lea spoke quietly. She maintained eye contact, concentrating as if she were following instructions on empathy from a self-help guide.

"Not think, not expect, not hope. You are positive that if I get you to the surface of Mars you can work out what killed everyone?"

"Yes." She sat forward. "I can." She squeezed his arm. "I'm sorry. You've been a big help."

Oswald checked on the progress of the exit scan, ignoring her clumsy apology. The clearance had been sent. He started his pre-flight procedure. "How long will it take you with what we have onboard now?"

"They made me leave my samples and some of my tools, in case they were contaminated." Lea sat back in her seat and threw her hands up.

"But the equipment on the shuttle. There are backups of everything right?"

"The shuttle itself can replace some of the portable equipment. It's a bit of a hassle, but that's what it was built for. It's hard to say." She bit her lip and closed her eyes.

"Best guess." Oswald brought up several flight paths and traced them with a finger. He punched in some rough calculations, focusing on the task instead of how difficult it would be to achieve.

"Could be a few hours to find the cause, but it may take weeks of testing to get proof."

"Let's hope hours, because there's no way we're gonna get weeks." Oswald switched the pickups back on.

The voice came through the ship's comm. "I say again shuttle. Comply with departure protocol or we will be forced to bring you back in for another decontamination and we will call the authorities."

Oswald heard the strain in the message. He figured the base staff was as fed up with Lea and himself as he was with them.

"Sending verification." Oswald punched in the codes, letting the computer take over the procedure.

**

It took twenty more minutes to get the okay to launch.

Lea rocked in her seat. "They dragged it out to punish us."

"It doesn't matter now." Oswald pulled the ship away from the moon. He was impressed with how calm she was.

"What are you going to do?" Lea rubbed her legs.

"We're going to Mars." He split his focus on his course and the thrust.

"They're never going to approve it."

Oswald flew to the first buoy that marked the approved route to Earth and launched the ship off course. "We're about to write our own ticket."

As soon as they were free from the sensors, Oswald sped up the shuttle and they headed to Mars at full speed. There were no official flight paths there, but he had studied what he could and knew how to get there, even if it wasn't the best window.

"Should be there by morning. We have to get there before they realize what we're up to. As soon as they figure it out they'll send everything they have to stop us."

Lea turned to face him. "Hey." She grabbed him. "You don't have to do this for me."

"I know. I still don't know what we're going to do when we get there. I've heard the monitoring satellites have automated defenses. Might just be a rumour to keep people away." Oswald watched for Lea's reaction.

She nodded and took out her tablet.

"You may want to get some sleep." He set the radio to scan for beacons and monitoring equipment.

"Too much to do. I've been planning a study on Mars for years, but I expected a full dome and all the time I wanted." She flipped through screens faster than Oswald could read them.

"I'll do my best to get you there. The rest is up to you."

Lea didn't respond. He checked the course he'd set and double-checked the fuel supply. When he was sure they were able to make the trip, he studied all the info he had on the blockade at the red planet.

***

According to their time relative to Lea's lab on Earth, it was late, not that the dark, star-speckled sky meant anything. The ship was silent. Oswald daydreamed about what they would discover on Mars. He kept finding a hidden, thriving community in his mind but would pull himself back to the abandoned colony and dead bodies he knew awaited them.

His imagination drifted between terrifying scenes of mass plagues and suffering people, monsters from the sky burning settlements, raising up the red ground to swallow structures whole, or tearing open the domes to the fledgling atmosphere and the people slipping into unconsciousness.

He shook himself into the present and pushed the monsters to the back of his mind. They closed the distance to the dead planet and the dangerous, illegal goal they gave themselves. Oswald went over what he knew about the perimeter again and rubbed his hands.

Lea hadn't put down her tablet. She kept him updated on her tasks and managed to get a tremendous amount done. Her eyes were red. She yawned and rubbed them then went back to the tablet.

Oswald wanted to comment on her dedication but didn't want to disturb her work. He stretched his back and stifled a yawn of his own. He had flown long flights before, but Mars was far from the moon and the asteroids pulled near to Earth for mining.

The planet was still a small orb in a black cloak when the ship reached the outermost ring of defense satellites.

The computer registered the automated devices, adjusting to the trajectory Oswald plotted through them. The ping-back came with a standard warning that Oswald ignored. "We're here."

Lea looked up and blinked. "Where?"

"Within range. We should be able to see the perimeter in a sec." He took hold of the controls, ready to adapt to any change.

Lea went back to the tablet, her fingers flying across the surface.

He held their course. Anticipating any threats, he kept his hand over the throttle. They sped on and the planet quickly took up the whole screen. A haze of weak atmosphere obscured the view.

The sensor screen showed the known position of the quarantined boundary and superimposed the orbits of the satellites and beacons Oswald had researched.

As they closed in, the planet's gravity pulled at the ship, and Oswald didn't slow down. Hundreds of objects circling the planet at varying heights changed from specks to dots to clear devices.

They held her breath. If any of the satellites were armed with more than EMP, they would be dust before they reached the atmosphere.

Oswald set the computer to scan the cloud of objects and moved the ship steadily forward. He watched the orbiting machines as they whipped past, trying to see any change.

"That's it." He smiled and breathed out a rush of air when they passed the marked perimeter.

Lea jumped, dropping the tablet. "What?" She scanned the cockpit frantically.

"I think we're going to make it." He faced her, keeping one hand on the controls. "Nothing seems to be going on out there. Any weapon would have shot us down before we got this close."

The shuttle shook violently. Oswald hit his head against a cushioned bulkhead and bit his cheek. His vision went fuzzy. Smoke streamed out of a panel and sparks shot out of a blown fuse. Screens and lights went out as the ship lost power.

"What hit us?" Lea reached back and strapped herself into the seat.

Oswald held his head in one hand and kicked the smoking panel open. Blood leaked out of his mouth as he spoke, staining his teeth. "Nothing—I don't know." He yanked at the controls, but they didn't respond.

"It must have been something!" Lea fished her tablet from the floor and switched it on, but it remained dark. She tried again then discarded the device. Straining against the straps, she looked through the small windows out front and on either side of the cockpit. "There must be an electromagnetic shield surrounding—the whole planet, I think."

"That's impossible." Oswald struggled to keep the shuttle on course, but the systems were still dead. He ripped off the metal panel covering the limited hydraulic controls as the planet pulled at the ship. "The power needed to cover a whole planet would be astronomical."

"It's right there." Lea pointed at a shimmer that followed the rounded horizon of the planet, but Oswald concentrated on flying. "I don't know how, but that's what got us."

"Hold on. We're gonna crash, but maybe I can keep us upright." He grabbed levers above his head, controlling movable panels on the outer hull of the ship and pulled hard.

The impact with the electromagnetic shield sent the ship spinning and changed their trajectory. Oswald fought to point them in the right direction, but they hit the atmosphere at a sharp angle. The front of the shuttle lit up with the friction, but it slowed the spin of the ship. He corrected, overcorrected, and then found the right angle to keep the ship from falling too fast. He grunted at the movement. Sweat ran down his face. He bared his teeth with every adjustment of the controls.

Straining, he reached over and hit a bright red emergency button under a thin pane of glass. Tiny shards stung his hand, but fuel sprayed out of the ship's tail, forcing it to keep steady.

Oswald's mind briefly wandered to Lea sitting beside

him. He was amazed at her composure. She dug under the control panel, pulling at wires, stripping some of them.

The atmospheric entry burned off most of the ship's front shielding, and the cabin was hot. Oswald focused on their falling, ignoring the sweat dripping in his eyes.

He yelled, but couldn't hear over the howl of their descent. He fully opened the hydraulic flaps, fighting the resistance, and they jerked forward. The stick dug into his stomach, knocking the wind out him. He heard Lea huff as the flaps caught more of the thin air and slowed the ship. Panels and pieces ripped free and tumbled away. He risked a glance towards Lea and saw blood. He couldn't see where she was hurt while he focused on their mad fall.

Lea sat upright. "I think I got it. Reboot the system."

He let go of one of the levers and snapped a series of switches up and down. The engine kicked on, and the ship blinked, flashed, beeped, and shuddered. The ship drifted when he let it go. He wrenched at the handle again, trying to steady their plummet.

The flickering monitor showed the position of the colony's domes as they screamed by them, overhead. Oswald saw their rough position and tried to find the aquifer, hoping for a water landing. He knew it was east of the domes, and that was roughly where they were. The huge domed lake of liquid water was already behind them and he searched for another place to bring down the shuttle. They limped across the sky, barely under control, losing altitude quickly.

The engines powered up enough for Oswald to switch to the regular control stick, but their speed, and the damage from the fall through the atmosphere, limited the ship's movement.

Lea reached over and pulled at the loose harness attached to Oswald's seat. "Strap in!"

A mountain came into view directly in their path. Oswald managed to turn away from it, but the momentum kept the shuttle moving along the same path. It collided with an outcropping and flipped end over end before it struck the mountain and rolled down to the surface.

Oswald reached out in a pathetic attempt to hold Lea in her seat. Her straps managed the task, and his arm smacked off of the console instead. As they bounced around, Oswald clenched his teeth to avoid biting off his tongue. He leaned back and pushed against the controls to keep himself pinned to his seat. With his jostling under control, he checked Lea. She was still bleeding, but was conscious and screaming. Oswald joined her as they tumbled.

When the ship came to a stop, they faced the ground. Oswald lay across the cockpit console and Lea dangled from her seat restraints.

"Ow." Oswald used the bulkhead to pull himself to a seated position.

Lea didn't move. He touched her face and shuffled under her to get a look.

"You all right?" He turned away from her and coughed. Specks of blood splattered the small window.

"My neck hurts. I don't want to move in case I make it worse." She gritted her teeth and winced when he touched her.

Oswald pushed himself up against the curve of the hull and felt her neck. "Everything seems to be where it should be." He grabbed her hands and feet. "Feel that?"

She nodded then winced again. "That's comforting. I take it you're still alive?"

"I'm pretty sure." Oswald dropped back and fell against the ruined instruments of the ship. The flight stick jammed into his back. His left arm was cut in a few places, and he felt a lump protruding from his head.

"I want to say something about your flying, but I suspect

it's the reason we're still alive." She slowly moved her head around and grunted at the pain.

"Don't thank me just yet. I have some bad news."

"We're on the wrong planet?" Lea rubbed her neck.

"The crash was more than the capsule was designed to take. The hull is cracked and we're leaking atmosphere. We lost some of it in the fall." Oswald moved under Lea and hit the release on her seat. She dropped, knocking the wind out of him. "Sorry." He coughed out the word.

"No." Lea shook her head then scrunched her face, squeezing Oswald's arm.

"I don't suppose you can think of a way out of this?" He put his uninjured arm around her.

"Maybe."

"What?" Oswald jerked forward, jostling Lea.

She grimaced. "The atmosphere. I took readings as we fell. It's still thin and there is way too much argon and carbon monoxide. It's poisonous, but just outside the tolerances to support life."

"So we'll die slowly? Assuming the reading was finished before the sensors were burned out in the descent."

"The terraforming. They bungled it somehow. Probably a malfunction or design flaw from the start. That's likely what killed everyone. They suffocated on the argon. Either way, it did enough for what we need."

"What does that mean for us?" Oswald felt a slick warmth on his chest. He slid his hand between himself and Lea and it came out red. He held her.

"If any of the masks and oxygen tanks survived the crash, you can probably make it to the domes."

"And you?" Oswald lifted Lea enough to look her in the eyes.

"Broken leg, probably a concussion."

"The blood?" He let her back down.

"I'm not going to make it."

"You'd better try. I don't want to die on Mars, and you're the one who's going to figure out a way off this planet." Oswald rolled Lea onto the canopy and tore off the flight stick to make a splint for her leg. He cut the straps from her seat restraint and used a piece of his shirt as a compress to stop her bleeding. Once she was treated to the best of his ability, he climbed into the cargo compartment, huddling his torn arm close to his chest, to find the oxygen.

He fed the tanks and masks into the cockpit. "One tank still functional. There are two masks, but one is cracked." He handed Lea the good one.

"No. You need that one." She weakly pushed the mask away.

He moved to put it over her head. "You're hurt, and I can hold my breath longer."

"You need to see where we're going. I can't lead you." She coughed and trembled at the convulsion. She groaned slightly and her head lolled back.

Oswald steadied her head and shook her. She snapped awake.

He relented, taking the good mask off her and putting the cracked one over her face. He connected the tank with a click and a small hiss. "We'll have to switch the tank between us."

Lea made some quick calculations, marking numbers with her blood on the canopy. "I think we can make it. The mountain isn't too far from the aquifer."

Oswald put on a bulky coat, carefully pushing his left arm through, and helped Lea into hers. The movement caused more blood to leak through the soaked fabric over her abdomen. He cinched her coat tight, ignoring her wincing. "Got to keep you in one piece. This isn't going to be any fun."

He nodded to Lea and pressed the airlock button. Nothing happened. He braced against the hatch and pushed. The seal cracked and the cabin atmosphere rushed out, replaced with red dust and cold toxic air. Wind blew across the open plain, making it difficult to see. Lea pointed to where the domes should be in the distance and put an arm over Oswald's shoulder.

He carried her forward and slung the tank over his other shoulder, ignoring the pain in his arm. The hose came loose, and he fumbled to connect it back to her mask.

They stumbled in the low gravity, but carrying Lea was easier than it would have been on Earth. Oswald adjusted, and they moved as quickly as he could manage. Maintaining his balance was difficult, though, and he tripped on the protruding rocks hidden in the blowing red sand, falling frequently.

Struggling to breath, even in the mask, he gasped. It burned his nose and eyes. Lea took charge of the oxygen, switching the hose. Oswald grunted and huffed forward and noticed he spent more time with it than she did. He was too concerned with getting them to safety to complain.

He bounded forward, dragging Lea as much as carrying her, moving steadily. They ran out of oxygen with the aquifer in sight. Oswald figured they were a kilometer away and ran, holding his breath, pulling Lea along with him. His chest ached and smoldered and started to convulse and his resolve broke. He knew the air was toxic, but his body fought for it. Breathing in made him choke and cough. He felt lightheaded and wavered. He gagged and spat and burned. Forcing his eyes to stay open, he blinked away tears.

Lea went limp in his arms, and Oswald heaved her over his shoulder. Through his mask he saw wet dust collected on her chest.

He ran into the wall of the clear dome and fell, dropping her. Through the dust, pain, and tears, he searched for an opening, feeling along the smooth surface for a break. The dome was huge and he couldn't spend any more time looking for an entrance.

Lea had stopped moving and Oswald's body rocked with spasms, screaming for air. His vision blurred. He felt around the ground, in the dust, and found a rock big enough to break the hard clear shell around the aquifer. It took dozens of swings, and he cut his hand, but he broke through. He went back to find Lea and fell. He breathed in again and vomited in his mask but it was enough for him to grab Lea and pull her into the safety of the dome.

He pulled off his mask and took a big, deep breath, hoping the life support could compensate for the hole in the side, but the air in the dome was as foul as outside. His head spun. He fell, panting, and reached out to touch Lea. His fingers were numb. Through the burning he saw the dome arch overhead. The air was thick with swirling sand, and his vision was blurred, but he noticed a huge, jagged hole in the top of the structure. Something, either pieces of the asteroid they'd intentionally sent to the surface, parts of the broken ship, or something he would never know, had broken through. Ferocious winds blew noxious air into the aquifer, carrying red dust in through the hole, collecting in the acrid water and covering their bodies.

Oswald pulled Lea close to him, but she did not move. He held his breath as long as he could. Spots swam in his dust clouded vision, spreading into darkness. His head felt inflated and squeezed by the air around him. Coughing, his breath leaked out. He desperately gasped in the thin, wretched atmosphere. The poisonous air filled his lungs, and he passed out.

The winds of Mars covered them in the light, red dust.

Digital Heaven

Digital Heaven
Christian Laforet

Juniper stood over the waterlogged body of her three year old son, Wesley. When talking to her friend, Suze, she'd noticed the boy was no longer playing at the edge of the fountain. Panic-stricken, she rushed over to find him face down in the shallow water. Juniper pulled him from the fountain and laid him before her. His delicate features were even more pronounced due to the fresh paleness of his skin.

The crowd, which formed around her, burst into applause. Juniper looked over to find a family standing directly to her left. The dad gave her a toothy smile before offering her a thumbs-up.

She couldn't take the inaction any longer and knelt at her son's side. Despite having no training in how to resuscitate a drowned person, she knew she had to try. Pounding his chest with one hand, Juniper used the other to lift his head, his wet hair becoming entangled in her fingers. She breathed into his open mouth. In her youth, she'd seen an old movie once where a person performed CPR. She hoped the film had been accurate.

The applause around her ceased. Although focused on Wesley, Juniper could hear one of the kids with the nearby family ask the mother, "What's that lady doing?" The mom's reply was snarky and loud. "She's denying that boy Paradise." Juniper didn't care. Paradise might be waiting for everyone, but she wasn't ready to let her son go.

She began puffing another lungful of air into his mouth when he jerked and coughed, water bubbling up past his lips. Yanking him into a sitting position, she furiously patted his back. Once his lungs were clear, the toddler began to cry.

"You should be ashamed of yourself!" The onlooker who spat the words towards her shook his fist disapprovingly as the rest of the crowd dispersed.

***

She decided to call a taxi for a ride home. Even though Wesley seemed okay, walking was not an option. Once they entered, the cab pulled off the curb and rose into the sky. It was a clear day and the traffic was light. Juniper could see most of the city from her seat. Pristine buildings and houses, like her own home, peeked from between the manicured trees lining the streets. Despite being one of the largest cities on the East Coast, there were fewer than a hundred thousand people, and from her vantage point, the panorama of her hometown was completely visible.

Even though they were headed straight home, she knew Suze would have already called Ellen, Juniper's mother. Her actions in saving Wesley were bizarre enough for Suze's need to tell everyone. Ellen would be waiting by the door for them to return, and Juniper would get an earful from the woman.

The taxi dropped them in front of their house. A disembodied voice came from hidden speakers. It reminded her the fare was already deducted from her account, and then, in a more pleasant octave, wished her and Wesley a fine day. With her son's head slumped on her shoulder and his arms slung loosely around her neck, Juniper started up the walkway to the house. The place belonged to Ellen, but after Juniper's husband, Thomas, died, she and Wesley had moved in. Careful not to wake Wesley, she slowly climbed up the front stairs. Just as she cleared the final step, the front door burst open.

"Hi, Mom," Juniper said, as she pushed past the woman.

"Oh, is that it? Is that all you have to say?" Her mother spun to follow her into the house. "Isn't there something you want to tell me?"

Juniper did not respond. Instead, she slipped her shoes off and quietly padded across the carpet towards Wesley's room. Once the boy was changed, tucked into his bed, and the door to his room closed behind her, she addressed her mother.

"You weren't there. It was too horrible. I couldn't just let him die." Juniper knew what she was saying would fall on deaf ears.

Her mother, never one to disappoint, waved her hand as if to discard every word which came out of Juniper's mouth as nonsense. "Oh, I understand all right, Juniper. I understand that you just robbed your son of Paradise."

Juniper stopped walking and faced her mother. "C'mon, Mom, I think you're being a bit overly dramatic. It's not like I made it so he can never die. When it's his time, Paradise will still be there."

Ellen turned towards a shelf lined with pictures and slid her finger across one in particular, a young couple holding a newborn. "I just wonder what Thomas would say about all this?"

Juniper felt her blood rise. "That's not fair." She jabbed a finger towards the photo. "Thomas could have seen Wesley every goddamn day if he had wanted to. Instead, he was so eager to go to Paradise, he left us all behind."

Thomas and Juniper had married young. She was barely into her twenties when Wesley was born. Their little family was a happy one—or so Juniper had thought. Thomas had always been obsessed with Paradise, even when they were kids, so it was no surprise when the call came to congratulate Juniper that her husband, the father of her child, had decided to use one of the many Ascension booths located throughout the city to end his life.

Apparently realizing she may have crossed a line, Ellen retreated from the shelves and the photographic memories they held, and began rearranging the pillows on the nearby couch. "Of course, honey, you know that's not what I meant."

"Yeah? What did you mean, then?" Juniper felt her voice falter as her emotions threatened to get the better of her.

"I'm just saying," her mother refused to make eye contact as she spoke, as if the conversation was barely worth her time, "you need to realize what the effect of doing something so…crazy, has on the rest of us. What do you think people are going to say when word gets around that you denied Wesley Paradise? We'll be pariahs! You know how people treat the Walkers down the street."

Juniper had to admit her mother had a point. People in their neighbourhood, although well-meaning, could be vicious towards anybody who thought differently. The Walker family was the perfect example. They used machines to keep their father alive for years and they were reviled because of it. Juniper went to school with one of the old man's kids before they had to be removed from classes due to the threat of violence against them. She'd witnessed firsthand what making a selfish decision like staving off death could mean in their society.

Dismissing her mother's comments, as well as her own contemplations, Juniper rested her hand on Ellen's shoulder, causing the older woman to turn away from her busywork. "I doubt we'll have to worry about that, Mom. People will just think I was caught up in the moment. It's not like I go around reviving my son every day."

"Well, I guess it can't be helped, you can't undo it," her mother conceded. "Now, before all this nonsense came up, I was going to call you and ask if you could stop at Frees Pharmacy on the way home. My pills came in."

Juniper shook her head. Of course her mother's pills would come in on the day she saved her son's life. "Okay. Do you want me to go get them for you?"

"No…you don't have to."

Juniper rolled her eyes. "It's fine. I'll go get them. Keep an eye on Wesley while I'm gone. He was shaken up pretty badly."

"Of course. I'll see if he's hungry when he wakes up."

Juniper sighed. Her mother hated going out. Partially because the woman was notoriously lazy, but the real reason, Juniper knew, was because Ellen always felt people were judging her on her age; few people made it to their sixties anymore. It had become such a problem that, even though her mother was still clearly upset over the morning's events, Ellen was willing to let it go if it meant saving her a trip to the pharmacy. In the end, Juniper felt like it was a good idea. She could use some time to clear her head.

It was still early, and Frees was not far, so she decided to walk. Her route took her directly past the Walker house. Two security units stood patrol on the lawn. She knew if she took a step onto the property, the units would activate. They would give her one warning before they removed her by force. It was pretty rare to see anybody employ such extreme measures for personal safety, but she supposed if any family needed the protection, it was the Walkers.

In one of the second floor windows, an ancient looking

man appeared and leaned towards the glass. Juniper felt her breath catch in her throat at the sight of him. Even with the daylight reflecting off the pane, she could see the tubes running to his nose, draped across the robe hanging from his bony shoulders. A shudder ran through her body. Everybody knew the old man was up there, but it was quite rare to ever see him. A sense of perversion overtook her. The thought of a person going to such extremes to stay alive sent a shiver across her body. She quickly looked away and hurried along to Frees. After a few steps, she glanced back over her shoulder, but the angle had changed and she couldn't see if he was still there. She imagined he was, watching her.

Juniper's neighbourhood sat just outside the city core. Within three blocks she'd crossed from family homes with manicured lawns to small business and public facilities. She passed few pedestrians along the way as most people used the various modes of transportation readily available throughout the city. Those she did meet, though, offered a pleasant smile or salutation. Since the advent of Paradise, some hundred years previous, the world's population had dwindled to just under a billion. Living in a city designed to house ten times its current population made for a lot of empty streets. The sidewalks were clear of any litter, the sky free of pollution. The only reason she knew such things existed at all was thanks to an excitable history teacher she'd had in grade school. The man took great joy in revealing such dirty things from mankind's past. He especially liked talking about crime. Juniper could remember being equally enthralled and terrified learning of such concepts as rape and murder. These things just did not exist in her world. There was no crime to speak of. Why steal? Why kill? You could leave all this behind whenever you wanted and go right to heaven.

Frees had existed as a staple of the neighbourhood for as long as Juniper could remember. She had fond memories of walking over to the pharmacy with her mother to use the parcel transport machine or to pick up various prescriptions. She smiled when the brass bell, a tarnished ball much older than she was, tinkled as she walked in. The pleasant sound was not loud enough, however, to interrupt the argument taking place at the counter.

"I've told you before, I'm not comfortable with ordering this stuff for you." Juniper recognized the pharmacist's voice before she could actually see him.

"What do you care?" The challenge came from a woman who appeared not much older than Juniper.

The pharmacist's expression went from annoyance to anger. "Listen, we all know why you want this stuff. I'm not one to tell people how to live their lives, but what you and your family are doing to your father is disgusting."

"I'm sorry, I thought you wanted our money? If you have such a big problem with me and my family, I would be happy to take my business somewhere else."

If the woman was bluffing, it failed. "I would be happy if you did just that," the pharmacist answered.

The lady spun and headed for the door. She brushed past Juniper, tears rolling down her cheeks.

The pharmacist wasn't finished yet. "If your family is so against letting people Ascend, why don't you move out to one of the uncovered zones and leave the rest of us alone?"

She waited until the door closed behind the woman before approaching the counter. It was an awkward moment, one which left Juniper at a loss for words.

Luckily, the pharmacist took the initiative and broke the silence. "I'm terribly sorry for the scene. I'm a tolerant guy, but some things really steam me good."

"Yeah…" She had no intention of asking what the argument was about, but the man was eager.

"My parents taught me to be a respectful person, but the

things that family is doing to that man…well, I don't even want to imagine it!"

Finally grasping who the woman had been, Juniper turned her attention to the front door. "Was that one of the Walkers?"

Nodding, the man behind the counter let out an exasperated sigh. "Why anybody would want to deny a person Paradise is beyond me. Anyways, enough of all that negativity. How can I help you?" A welcoming smile spread across his face.

Reaching her hand out so the DNA scanner could identify her, Juniper eyed the man. What would he think of her if he knew she'd resuscitated her son earlier in the day? "I'm here to pick up my mother's Ascension pills."

Reading the display flashing between them, the man's smile widened. "Oh, yes, I was hoping I would see you today. I have your mother's prescription right here. I have to say, I was really excited to get them in. Most people around here are content with the run-of-the-mill Ascension pills, and that's fine if you just want a good, clean and…boring death. Am I right?" The man, resting his folded arms across the counter, gave Juniper a wink.

"I guess." Something about the man's tone made her skin crawl.

"Boy! When I got this order, I said to myself, 'Self, this is a person with some real style, right here'." As he spoke, the pharmacist typed in some numbers. Seconds later, a small bottle of pills appeared on the parcel transport pad to the left of the counter. "I'm really envious of your mother, you know?"

"Well…" Juniper motioned around the store towards the various displays of pills and devices dedicated to killing oneself.

The man let out a laugh. "I know, I know. But I promised my wife I would wait until the kids are out of high school before I Ascend."

Juniper forced a smile and gave a friendly nod which she hoped read as, I hear ya.

After surviving some small talk about the weather, Juniper managed to escape Frees with her mother's prescription in hand. She turned the bottle of pills over, the few within rattling around. Only one pill was needed to Ascend, but just in case, the company who made them included a couple of extras. She remembered how excited her mother had been when she read about them. Ellen had been planning her sixtieth birthday and Ascension party for nearly four months. Most people Ascended long before sixty. Even amongst her friends, Ellen was the oldest. The common practise was to wait until your children had children of their own, or at the very least, reached adulthood, and then Ascend. Thanks to Thomas going early, Ellen had put off her own Ascension for a couple of years to help Juniper with Wesley.

The pills were a premium European brand promising a quick, euphoric death. The advertisements, which Ellen would quote from at least three times a week, stated the patented formula also affected the body. There would be no messy clean-up from evacuated bowels, and on top of that, a chemical compound in the pills would tighten the skin, removing all wrinkles. Indeed, the slogan for the pills was: You may be old, but you can still leave a young looking corpse.

Even though Juniper had been to several Ascension parties, she'd never attended one for an immediate family member. When Thomas killed himself, it was an impromptu event. Her father died without any help at all. He'd suffered a heart attack.

Once Ellen was gone, Juniper and Wesley would be left with no one but each other. It wouldn't be easy. Shaking her head, she stuffed the prescription back into the small, white paper bag it came in and walked away from the pharmacy.

Not ready to return to home, Juniper began to wander the city. The morning had been a stressful one. She was still conflicted over saving Wesley's life. She knew in her heart she'd made the right decision, but her brain kept insisting it was a selfish one. Lost in her own thoughts, she barely noticed the young couple pass by. When the dog they were walking let out a shrill yap, it nearly scared her half to death. Glancing around, Juniper realized she had walked farther from her house then she'd intended. Shops and restaurants she'd never seen before stood out around her. This area of the city was more crowded than most. She found it comforting to be surrounded by so many people. They smiled as they passed each other, some sparking up conversations.

Though she had never been to that particular area of the city, Juniper wasn't actually lost. It was impossible for most people—including Juniper—to lose their way, as the communication chip, which was inserted behind the right ear shortly after birth, included a fully functional GPS system. The practice of chipping, as they called it, really took off during her mother's generation, and since there were not too many people around these days older than Ellen, it meant almost everybody had one.

After a while, the trendy shops melted away, and she strolled into one of the forgotten sections of the city. Because of the small populations, the bigger cities had several nearly abandoned areas. These usually appeared around hospitals and other medical facilities. As she walked on, she spied the top of one such building in the distance. Because all maintenance was taken care of mechanically, these areas and structures remained in good shape. In fact, it was most likely that the hospital was exactly as it had been a century earlier when it was still needed. Juniper briefly entertained the idea of heading towards the empty building but decided she should start home instead. As she rounded the block, she passed a church.

Churches, unlike hospitals, had been modified in the last hundred years. Every single church, temple, and mosque around the globe was repurposed—converted—into something much more closely resembling a museum.

Juniper stared at the church for several minutes before walking up the steps. She feared the large wooden doors might be locked, but managed to pull one of them open with a hefty tug.

The interior exhibited an exercise in simplicity. She had seen pictures of churches back in grade school history class, but most of what she recalled about them had been stripped away. Where she suspected stained glass windows had once decorated the walls was now a collection of plastered-over arched indents. Walking down the aisle, she passed between a dozen rows of padded benches to reach a non-descript, grey altar. Floating over it was a fist-sized orb.

On the whole, churches were useless things. She did not know a single person who visited them on any sort of regular basis. As far as she was concerned, their only purpose was as a destination for children on field trips.

When she neared the orb, it lifted a foot higher into the air, a warm glow emanating from it.

"Hello, information seeker. What may I tell you about Paradise?"

"I don't know…why the hell are we all in such a hurry to get there?" Juniper let out an amused chuckle. Why had she even come here? Shaking her head, she turned to leave.

"Before Paradise, people were dying at an alarming rate."

Juniper smiled as she faced the orb once more. Her question had only been rhetorical. "That's pretty funny. It seems like that's exactly what people are doing right now."

The orb's AI obviously could not process Juniper's response. Instead, it opted to follow some kind of default programming and began explaining the process which led to the creation of Paradise. "In the year 2107, humankind made a scientific breakthrough. Using cutting-edge technology, we were finally able to follow a person into death. A question as old time was going to be answered. What happens when we die? Celebration shifted to despair when the first bits of data began coming back. All of the evidence supported the same conclusion. There is no afterlife. The human race was thrown into turmoil. The sudden realization that all religious belief was a lie bore a devastating impact.

"Riots broke out across the world. Whole cities burned. Millions perished. For nearly fifty years, all hope was lost. We've come to call this period, The Time of the Great Truth.

"Humankind was on the verge of self-annihilation. The remaining Earth governments worked together to prevent just such a thing from happening, and a solution was reached. If heaven was not real, then it would have to be created.

"The Paradise initiative was launched in 2159. Nearly a thousand satellites were sent into orbit around the Earth. These satellites were programed with state of the art technology which could read, and collect, a human's energy upon death. Every man, woman, and child was now assured a place in Paradise when they passed."

Juniper had heard it all before. There was not a single person alive who had not learned the history of Paradise, even a hundred years after its launch. Deciding to have some fun with the device, she pointed her index finger toward the orb and asked, "All right, smart guy, then tell me this? How do you know Paradise actually works?"

"Please re-state your question, believer."

Laughing, Juniper rested on the corner of one of the benches. "You heard me. What if we get there and Paradise doesn't even work?"

This time, without missing a beat, the voice replied, "The minds behind the creation of Paradise were the brightest of their time. The technology is sound. Rest assured, when the time comes to Ascend, Paradise will be awaiting you."

Juniper made a face at the non-answer. She hadn't expected anything too deep from the orb, anyway. "What if I don't want to go to Paradise?"

For a moment, the orb spun silently in place. Apparently, the machine did not have a response as it said, "In the year 2107, humankind made a—"

"Shut up. Okay, try this, if Paradise is for everybody, why are there still uncovered zones?"

Again with the spinning. This time, though, the orb had an answer. "The Paradise satellites cover ninety-eight percent of the globe. Because of the Earth's magnetic resonance, and as a result of solar activity, the remaining two percent remains uncovered. These portions are called the uncovered zones. In recent years, steps have been taken to account for these interferences, and based on the most current projections, the uncovered zones will be reduced to zero percent in the next two to five years."

Juniper let the information set in for a moment. "Where is the nearest uncovered zone?"

The orb began spinning even faster before coming to an abrupt stop. "This unit does not have the necessary information to adequately answer your inquiry."

Having heard enough, Juniper headed for the doors. Behind her, the lights in the church dimmed. Glancing back, she noted that the orb had reset itself to its starting position just above the altar.

***

When Juniper returned home, she found Wesley playing with his toys on the front porch.

"Momma!"

As she embraced her son, all thoughts of having made the wrong decision in saving his life evaporated.

"You were gone for a long time."

Juniper glanced up as her mother spoke to her from inside the screen door.

"I just kind of wandered, I guess. I see this little guy is feeling just fine."

Her mother joined them on the porch, her fingers sliding through the toddler's sandy-brown hair. "You know boys, they're hearty."

Love for Wesley was obvious in her mother's eyes. Juniper bit back the desperate plea which balanced on her tongue, and instead said, "I got your pills."

"Fantastic. When you didn't come home, I was worried maybe they hadn't come in after all and you'd had to search elsewhere." Ellen pulled the pill bottle from the bag and held it before her face like she was appraising a diamond, not admiring her method of suicide. "These are great. I'm going to be the envy of the neighbourhood."

"Yeah, Mom, everybody's going to be real jealous."

Her mother was too focused on the pill bottle to catch the sarcasm in Juniper's tone. "I know! I have to call Betty. She says if my death is as great as this company claims, she's going to make an order herself. Can you imagine that? Your mom is going to be the trendsetter around here."

Juniper watched Ellen disappear into the house before crouching next to Wesley, who had returned to his toys. "Hey, baby. How are you feeling?"

"Good," he said absentmindedly as he rammed a small metal car into the awaiting jaws of a T-Rex.

"Are you sure?"

He gave her an exasperated look. "I said I'm fine."

She laughed at the boy's recovered attitude. "Hey, you know what?"

"What?"

"I love you lots, kid." She ruffled his hair. "I'm sorry you didn't get to see your dad today."

Feeling a wave of emotion coming, she got up and headed for the front door. She was almost there when Wesley spoke.

"I did see Daddy."

Juniper stopped, her heart suddenly beating faster. "What did you say, honey?"

"You said I didn't get to see Daddy, but I did."

"You did?" She tried to keep her voice calm. "When?"

"Today. It was after I was playing in the water."

Juniper was speechless. Surely, she was reading too much into what the boy said. She licked her lips. "What…what did he say?"

Wesley picked up his toys and studied them, shifting them slowly in his hands. The expression on his face was a thoughtful one; clearly he was searching through his limited vocabulary to find the right words. "He was very sad, but not only sad…I think he was scared, too."

"What?" Juniper surprised herself by the alarm in her voice. "How do you know he was scared?"

"Because he was screaming."

Juniper's breath caught in her throat. "I don't understand what you mean, honey."

Wesley let his toys clatter to the porch "I tried to talk to him. I wanted to tell him I miss him, but he was screaming so loud…it hurt my ears." He pressed his palms against the sides of his head.

Picking up the toys, Juniper placed a comforting hand on her son's shoulder. "Maybe you're wrong. It was a really scary moment. Maybe you just think you heard Daddy."

Wesley knocked her hand away. "I know it was Daddy! He was in the white place and he was screaming!"

Juniper didn't know what to say. The conviction in her son's voice was unmistakable. He truly believed what he told her. Fighting a sudden wave of dizziness, Juniper ruffled Wesley's hair one more time before retreating into the house. She knew it was not a very motherly thing to do, leaving her son alone after what he'd revealed to her, but she couldn't help it.

She entered the kitchen, where her mother was humming as she prepared the evening meal. Juniper saw they were having Wesley's favourite for dinner: spaghetti.

"He's a strong kid, I'll give him that. He's just like his grandpa that way." Ellen smiled warmly as she stirred the sauce.

"Mom…did Wesley say anything to you?"

Her mother stopped her work and moved towards her. "Are you okay, honey? You look like you've just seen a ghost."

Resting against the counter in an attempt to remain steady, Juniper took a drink from the glass of wine Ellen had sitting there. "I'm fine. Just…please, did Wesley say anything…weird to you?"

Ellen's eyebrows knit as she put her hand on Juniper's shoulder. "Oh—you're shaking! What's going on?"

"Just tell me, Mom!"

"No…no, he hasn't said anything. Why, should he have?"

"It's nothing." Juniper emptied the glass before rubbing a hand across her forehead. "It's just been a crazy day." She knew Ellen would brush off the boy's comments as the work of an overactive imagination, then turn her attention to Juniper for getting so worked up over it in the first place. Better to keep it to herself.

Ellen stared thoughtfully for a moment before pouring Juniper another glass of wine. "I've been thinking…"

"Not now." Juniper knew anytime her mother started a sentence with 'I've been thinking', it was usually going to be something Juniper did not want to hear.

Retrieving a second glass from the cupboard, Ellen poured herself some wine. She took a long drink before pushing on with her thought. "I love you guys so much. You know that, right? And you know that all I've ever wanted was to have my family back again."

She gave her mother the hardest stare she could, but the woman either didn't notice or pretended not to see it.

"Just think how great it would be if we all went. Thomas, your dad, all of us together again."

Hearing Thomas' name brought Wesley's chilling words back to Juniper. "Stop it. Let's just eat dinner and get this awful day over with."

Ellen pulled the pills from one of the oversized pockets stitched into the front of her apron. "With these we could do it. We could all be a family again."

"I've asked you to drop it." Juniper pushed past Ellen, finishing her wine then slamming her empty glass into the sink. The delicate stem snapped off when it struck the bottom. "Shit!"

Rushing over to clean up the broken pieces, Ellen took on an apologetic tone. "You're right, I'm sorry. Now's not the time. We can talk about it tomorrow."

***

Juniper woke, covered in sweat. The blinds in her bedroom window sliced the morning sun into a half-dozen horizontal slashes that stretched across her room. She'd put Wesley to bed shortly after dinner the night before and followed suit after a much needed shower. However, her sleep was plagued by restless dreams. Nothing concrete remained of them besides a general feeling of unease which greeted her upon waking.

Thankfully, Ellen was already gone. One of the few things which could get Juniper's mother out of the house was the weekly Paradise breakfast. Several of the women in the neighbourhood who were planning on Ascending in the coming year would get together over pancakes and coffee and discuss important topics, like what they were going to wear when they killed themselves and whether or not they should tell people how they really felt about them before they left. Juniper was sure Ellen would be the centre of attention today, what with her fancy new pills and all.

Wesley was as chipper as could be. Any traumatic remnants of the previous day had been swept away with the night. Over breakfast, Juniper tried for a bit to broach the subject of Wesley's father, but he was much more interested in talking about why he loved cereal with marshmallows in it.

Three days a week, Wesley went to daycare. Juniper always walked him there, even though the daycare had a private bus service. A kiss on the head and a pat on the butt sent the boy racing into his classroom. One of the women who worked there waved politely at Juniper, but something about the look in her eyes gave Juniper a funny feeling.

As she made her way towards the front door, she could hear a couple of the staff talking. It was obvious by the sudden drop in tone and furtive glances that they were talking about her. Juniper sighed. She should have expected her actions the day before would have spread this far already.

Feeling her temper flare, Juniper tapped the spot behind her ear which activated her receiver—another perk of being chipped. "Call Suze."

A faint ringing sound bounced through her brain for a moment before an overly friendly voice answered. "Hey! How's Wesley doing?"

Juniper ground her teeth at Suze's tone. The receiver made the other woman's voice sound as if she was standing directly in front of her. "He's doing just fine. I just wanted to call and say thank you so very much for telling everybody in the city about what happened."

As Suze sputtered, Juniper continued, not giving her the opportunity to reply. "You're a real good friend, Suze."

"That's not fair. I was scared, okay? I didn't know what you were doing. I've…I've never seen anybody try and prevent a person from dying before. It seemed so—"

"Natural?"

"Disgusting."

Juniper shook her head. "You know what? How about you go fuck yourself."

A shocked huff came through the receiver. "End call." Juniper cut off whatever Suze was going to say. "Receiver, block all calls from Suze." A mild beep issued within her head, confirming her request.

Wesley would be in daycare until noon, which gave Juniper four hours to herself. Normally she'd head home, but she decided against it. Her mother usually spent the whole morning at her breakfast, but on the off chance she returned early, Juniper had no desire to deal with the dropped conversation from the night before. Instead, she grabbed a coffee from a nearby café and headed for the park.

Since the weather was satellite controlled, it was almost always a perfect day. Children ran wild across several jungle gyms, while parents drank coffee and chatted with each other from the safety of one of the dozens of park benches which lined the play area.

Juniper stared at all the smiling faces of the little ones. They were so happy. Not just the kids, either. Even the parents appeared to be enjoying the idea of just being there. Juniper couldn't help but think of her mother, Thomas, and every other person she knew who decided such a pleasant place was no longer for them. She was so deep in her own thoughts, she jumped when the woman standing behind her spoke.

"Excuse me?" When she turned to see who spoke, Juniper felt her stomach lurch. Although she did not know the woman's name, she certainly recognized her face. She'd seen her the day before at Frees Pharmacy.

"I said, 'They're all so carefree'."

Her mouth suddenly dry, Juniper nodded towards the woman. "Kids love it here. I bring my son here all the time."

The woman smiled and moved to stand next to Juniper. She tilted her head towards the children running and playing before them. "Which one is yours?"

"Oh, no, he's not here today. I was actually just killing time before I have to pick him up from daycare."

A brief silence descended between them before Juniper cleared her throat and said, "I think…I think I saw you yesterday at Frees."

A momentary flash of red brushed the woman's cheeks, and she looked away. "Yeah, that was unfortunate. So you know who I am, then?"

Juniper felt her face flush. "Well, I don't know you personally, but I know—"

"My family. Everybody knows the Walker family."

The woman appeared very sad. Juniper turned away, pretending something else had caught her eye.

"I suppose you want me to leave?"

"No, no, not at all." Juniper forced an awkward smile. "Uh…my name's Juniper, by the way." She thrust her hand out towards the woman.

The woman's eyes widened as she stared at Juniper's hand for a moment. Eventually, she shook it. "Kell."

"Well, it's nice to meet you, Kell."

Kell held her hand for a second longer than appropriate. "You know, it's been a long time since anybody has been happy to meet me." She finally released the grip when a tear rolled from the corner of one eye. "Look at me. I'm so embarrassed. I spend so much time trying to convince people that I'm not crazy, and then I meet a nice person and here I am, acting crazy."

Juniper let out a small laugh. "You know what? Lately, I

think we're all crazy."

"Tell me about it." Kell retrieved a tissue from her purse and wiped her eyes. "I come to this park almost every day and I can't help but marvel at how these people act."

"What do you mean?"

"Do you see them? They literally have no cares. They live in a perfect world, but do they even notice? Nope. All they care about is getting to Paradise as fast as possible."

It was odd for Juniper to hear somebody verbalise the thoughts she had been just having moments before. "So… what's wrong with Paradise?"

Juniper could see the woman go rigid. She couldn't imagine what it must be like to have so much hate thrown at you every time you opened your mouth. "I'm not judging. I really want to know."

Kell sighed. "Everybody's been duped, okay? The whole world has been served a lie, and we were all too happy to eat it up."

Even with her own doubts, Juniper found Kell's comments to be almost sacrilege. "I'm sorry. I'm not calling you a liar, but how could that be? Paradise has been around for so long, surely somebody would have found out."

Kell laughed. The sound was hollow, completely devoid of happiness. "That's the great trick, though, isn't it? You only learn the truth when you die. So unless you can actually find somebody who has been there and then come back, you'll never know."

Juniper felt her head spin as a single thought bounced around it like a cannonball. Wesley has.

***

For the rest of the morning, Juniper couldn't get the brief conversation with Kell Walker out of her head. She'd tried to get the woman to reveal more about Paradise, but, after their initial exchange, Kell clammed up. Shortly after, she mumbled something about packing boxes and left. Juniper watched her scurry away, casting paranoid glances towards every person she passed. Juniper shook her head in disbelief. It startled her how fast the things she believed in, the things she took for granted, could be so badly shaken. Worse—how easily, and with such little evidence. Yesterday morning, she'd accepted Paradise and all it promised, but after saving Wesley, his revelation of what awaited there and Kell Walker's startling words, she was left feeling alone and scared.

With heavy thoughts weighing down her mind, Juniper made her way home. She groaned when Ellen waved to her from one of the living room windows. Breakfast must have ended early.

"Oh good, you're home." Ellen hopped up from the couch excitedly as Juniper entered the house. "I have some big news."

Juniper nodded absentmindedly towards her mother. Her intention had been to use the couple of hours before Wesley finished daycare to do some digging online in regards to the history of Paradise. She had no idea what such a search would reveal, but she felt desperate. "That's good, Mom."

Seemingly unperturbed by Juniper's disinterest, Ellen gleefully launched into her big news. "So, you know how I was planning to Ascend next month for my sixtieth birthday?"

"Huh, oh, yeah…so?"

"Well, it appears that Monica from down the street is planning her own for the day before. She said something about her astrological sign. Can you believe that nonsense? Some people are so gullible. Anyway, it's pretty tacky to have an Ascension party within a week of a friend or family member's."

"I didn't know that Monica from down the street was a friend or family member?" Juniper laughed, despite her pre-occupied state.

"You know what I mean."

"Okay, so, what're you getting at?"

Ellen gently grabbed Juniper's shoulders and guided her over to the couch. When she was seated, Ellen clasped her hands together. "You know what this Saturday is, right?"

Juniper felt a tremor of worry bubble up in her stomach. "No…"

"This Saturday would be me and your father's fortieth anniversary. Since Monica already has her day booked, I thought what better time to be reunited with your dad than on the day we were married."

Juniper stared into her mother's smiling face. "Are you saying you're going to kill yourself this Saturday?"

"Uh huh."

"As in, three days from now?"

Ellen nodded excitedly.

Juniper stood, shaking her head. "You should get an award for worst timing ever." Pissed, she stormed off.

"Juniper? I thought you'd be happy for me."

"Happy?" Spinning back around, Juniper pointed a finger towards her mother. "You thought I'd be happy? It seems that the only person who will be happy is you, and, since you'll be dead, I doubt even that!"

"Juniper, don't talk that way."

With a humph, Juniper disappeared into her room, slamming the door behind her.

***

The next couple of days flashed by. Ellen was a whirlwind of activity, getting all her preparations in order for her Ascension. Juniper found it funny how the most energy she'd ever seen her mother exert was in the name of killing herself. Wesley was the same as ever, a happy little boy, his brief exposure to Paradise all but forgotten. Juniper envied the child. She wished she could unlearn the things she had, but every time she had a moment to herself, the doubts crept back in. She spent a great deal of time trying to learn everything she could about Paradise, and, although a great wealth of information existed on the subject, Juniper was surprised to learn none of it went deeper than what the church had told her the day before. There was nothing about how or why the satellites worked besides a small piece before the process became automated, published thirty years previous, about a manned mission to repair one of the satellites.

She considered heading over to the Walker house, but she always found a reason not to. She recognized she was avoiding them out of fear. There was still a part of her that wanted to, and still did, believe in Paradise. The thought of having the last string of hope severed frightened her.

***

Ellen was up early the day of her suicide. It annoyed Juniper to hear her mother humming and moving about like she was having the best day of her life. She wanted to shake the woman. When Ellen asked her to go to the store for some snacks and beverages, Juniper gladly agreed.

The only clouds in the brilliant blue sky appeared like giant streaks of paint across a cerulean canvas. Juniper took a deep breath of the fresh morning air and felt some of her irritation leave her. She tried to convince herself she had overreacted. For all she knew, Ellen would be celebrating her anniversary with her husband in Paradise by the end of the day.

As soon as she rounded the corner, she could hear a commotion. A group of people were gathered out front of the Walker home. Despite wanting to avoid the family at all costs, the scene piqued her curiosity and Juniper wandered over.

She approached a stout man standing at the edge of the crowd. "What's going on?"

"These savages are finally leaving." The man snorted with disgust before spitting on the sidewalk.

Juniper pushed past him. She could see a small loading craft hovering a few inches above the driveway.

The crowd was quite agitated. Several people yelled hateful slurs towards the occupants of the house.

Kell Walker burst out the front door. She pointed an accusing finger at the crowd. "You people are horrible! You should all be ashamed of yourselves."

Not wanting to be seen or associated with the mob, Juniper moved so the stout man was blocking her from Kell's view.

"Just leave us alone! What have we ever done that's so bad? Do you hate us because we love our father? Is that why you've made our lives hell?"

Juniper could hear the pain in her words.

A teenage girl threw a rock at Kell. "You're disgusting! You and your whole family shouldn't be allowed into Paradise."

The stone hit Kell in the shoulder and an uncomfortable smile spread across her face. It appeared all the more out of place framed by tears. "That's the nicest thing anyone has ever said to me. Paradise is bullshit and you're all going to burn there."

Kell's words whipped the crowd into a frenzy. Juniper was pulled towards the house as the mob surged forward. The shouting intensified, followed by more rocks and sticks. Kell quickly ducked back inside her home.

As the stones began pelting the house, the two security units stationed on the lawn came to attention. They swung in unison to face those encroaching on the property. "Desist all aggressive action towards this household," the machines commanded in stereo.

The threat of being physically removed by the security

units had the desired effect. The majority of the crowed cautiously backed away from the home. Juniper was surprised when the stout man who had been standing next to her moments before, heedless of the robots' warning, made a break for the front porch. A large metal fist collided with his chest, sending him rag dolling backwards into the crowd. The display was enough to hasten the angry mob's dispersal.

Juniper was soon alone in front of the house. She wanted to leave, but since she was already there, her mind insisted she take the final step. She started up the walkway to the front porch, but stopped suddenly when the security units directed their attention towards her. Heart racing, she backstepped off the property. "Excuse me? Hi." Still aware of some of the stragglers being close enough to hear her, Juniper tried to keep her voice low.

The front door opened a crack. "Don't you people take a hint? Oh…it's you." Kell Walker emerged onto the porch once again. "You weren't with them, were you?"

Juniper shook her head quickly. "No! No. I was just walking by and saw all the commotion."

"Well, what do you want?"

What did she want? Juniper felt like an idiot standing there. To make things worse, she could practically feel the attention of the other neighbours burrowing into her back, waiting to see what she would do next.

She had to know. "Is what you said true? About Paradise?"

Kell remained silent as her eyes darted between the stragglers still within sight of her home. Finally, she held out her hand. "If you want to know the truth, if you want to know exactly what Paradise is, then you'd better come in and talk to Father." Kell ordered the security units to stand down.

Juniper stared at the woman's open hand like it might be contagious. Then, despite the growing knot in her stomach, she slowly ascended the front steps and followed Kell Walker into her home.

Stacks of books and newspapers lined the walls. Juniper had never seen so much print material in all her life. Stopping to examine one of the many tomes, she was surprised to see, along with those on either side, that it appeared homemade. The Truth About Digital Heaven and They Promised Heaven But Gave Us Hell were just a couple of the titles decorating the bent and creased covers.

"My father's life's work." Kell grabbed one of the books, briefly leafed through it, and then tossed it back on top of the pile.

"Your father wrote all these?" Juniper spun in a circle to take in all the books. There had to be hundreds of them.

Kell laughed. "No! Dad couldn't write a book if his life depended on it. Nah, these all come from other people. Dad just collects them."

The anti-Paradise propaganda did not end with the books, either. Juniper noticed several faded posters, most of them damaged, clinging to the walls of the Walker house. She wondered why they were in such a poor state before she realized they were probably liberated from the sides of buildings. It was almost offensive to even imagine such a message being stuck out in public for all to see. One thing was certain, having just witnessed the levels of intolerance her neighbours displayed towards the Walkers, it would take somebody with some serious guts to actually post one of those things.

After retrieving a mug of something from her kitchen, Kell led Juniper up a flight of rickety stairs and through a narrow hallway. Only one door along the length was open and, as they neared it, she could see movement in the room.

A pang of nervousness set her stomach to knotting. Nearly her whole life, Juniper had been told how awful this family was—especially the patriarch, old man Walker. Now, she voluntarily entered his bedroom to listen to what he had to say.

The man was old. Probably the oldest person she had ever seen, but, as she made her way fully into the bedroom, she saw he was far from ancient. In fact, if not for his obvious poor health, he could easily be within ten years of Ellen.

The man appeared surprised when Kell and Juniper entered his space. Sitting on the side of his bed, he quickly stood up to face them. A machine stationed next to him started to tip with his effort, thanks to a half dozen wires protruding from its front side. Juniper saw the wires all snaked along the floor and then disappeared up the bottom of his robe.

"Daddy, calm down. It's okay." Kell rushed over and stopped the machine before it could topple.

"Who is this?" the man asked Kell. Before she could answer, he shifted his gaze towards Juniper. "Who are you?"

"I-I…"

"She's a friend, Dad." Kell placed a hand on the old man's shoulder.

Keeping his eyes on Juniper, the man seemed to relax a bit. "Well, why is she here?"

"This is Juniper. She's one of our neighbours. I talked to her the other day. She has some questions about Paradise."

Juniper tried her best to smile, but it didn't quite materialize. Reaching out a hand in greeting, she said, "It's nice to meet you, sir."

The man completely ignored her gesture. Instead, he grabbed a pair of glasses from a small mahogany end table next to his bed. With the spectacles balancing on the end of his nose, he took Juniper in.

"So, you have questions about Paradise, do you?"

Juniper nodded.

"Why?"

She launched into the events that recently took over her

life. Her eyes filled with tears that threatened to slide down her cheeks when she recounted Wesley's description of what awaited him in Paradise. She even included Ellen's planned Ascension.

With a long sigh, the man motioned towards a worn chair next to the window. "Please have a seat, my dear. I have a story to tell.

"First off, my name is Gabriel, and I have been fighting off death for the last thirty-six years. I wasn't sick back then, but, still, after what I learned, it seemed like a wise decision. Since life has a twisted sense of humor, I, of course, contracted a rare disease shortly after starting my efforts."

"It's funny. We have the means, as a race, to live for two or three lifetimes, yet we don't. Take my ailment, for instance. I have no doubt that it could be cured in a week—hell, a day, if the right minds were put to it. That isn't going to happen though. You want to know why? Because when things break, even people, we just throw them away. And that's okay, because there is always something waiting, whether it be more things or an artificial afterlife. In fact, there is only one thing that must be fixed at all costs. Do you know what that is?"

Juniper wanted to have an answer for the man, but her mind was blank. "I...I don't know."

With a soft chuckle that quickly became a hard cough, Gabriel answered for her, "Paradise."

Her hours of research came flooding back to her. During her reading on the subject, Juniper recalled the article reporting on the manned mission to fix one of the Paradise satellites.

Gabriel must have seen understanding light her eyes, as a wide smile slid across his face. "I was an astronaut when I was a much younger man. When mankind fabricated its own heaven, exploring the stars lost all its luster. But they still needed people who could go up there and fix the damn things, at least they still did back then."

"It was the thrill of a lifetime for me, I'll tell you that." Gabriel let his gaze fall past Juniper and settle on the window. "Nothing can prepare you for being in space. I've never felt so insignificant and yet so magnificent at the same time."

"What happened? When you were in space?"

"One of the satellites had been struck by a micro-meteor. The impact did not damage the system, but it was enough to throw it slightly off course. If we did not repair and re-orient it, within a year it would re-enter Earth's atmosphere.

"When we got up there, we started replacing the damaged panels. It was my job to access the satellite's computer system to make sure everything was still functioning."

Gabriel took a sip from a steaming mug Kell had brought him. Juniper couldn't tell for sure what the man was drinking, but it smelled like it might be some sort of herbal tea.

"Where was I? Oh yes, I was checking the satellite's computer system.

"Like most people, I was obsessed with Paradise, but not in the same way. The idea of a guaranteed afterlife was all fine and great, but how did the damn thing work? Everything I had ever read or been told about its creation was that it was a technological marvel, but never, not once, had I heard a single piece of information on the how's and why's of it all. That really got to me.

"I hooked up with some people with similar questions the year before my space trip. We theorized that with the right opportunity, we could create a program which would map, and, in a way, let us peek into the digital realm which awaited us all at death. You just needed access to the satellites."

Juniper nodded in understanding. "And there you were, in space, hooked up to one of them."

Gabriel took another drink from the mug, this time,

though, with a bit more gusto. Juniper could see talking about his experience was getting the man's blood up.

"Yes! Yes, exactly. So, there I am, floating in the absolute absence of everything with my sneaky little fingers in the Paradise pie."

"What did you find?" Juniper's excitement caused her to nearly jumble the question.

Gabriel remained quiet for a moment. He stared down at the mug in his hand as if contemplating another drink, but after a few seconds, negotiated it towards his end table. "I found out everything, my dear.

"The technology is actually sound, but there is a problem. When we die, one of those bloody technological marvels up there"—he thrust a finger towards the ceiling—"can snatch your consciousness before it fades, and, at the speed of light, transfer it into one of the awaiting servers. Now, that's all fine and good, but the real issue presents itself once you get there. Even with thousands of xenottabytes of space available in each satellite, a certain amount of compression has to happen to store the ever increasing data of human souls filling them. Think about that for a moment."

Juniper was having trouble keeping up with the man but did as he instructed. Although she couldn't imagine the processing power happening on any one of the Paradise satellites, she did know compressing files could lead to some level of corruption. If what Gabriel said was true, then the technology floating above them was collecting human consciousness and reducing it to a small digital size. The mere thought of it started her stomach churning.

Gabriel looked sad as he turned back towards his bed. Speaking as much to himself as he was Juniper, he said, "Those poor bastards had no idea. The torment they're in…"

She waited for more, but Gabriel appeared to be finished

with his history lesson. With a small wave of his hand towards his daughter, Kell grabbed Juniper's arm and led her from the bedroom.

"Is that true?" Juniper asked, as she craned over her shoulder to peer at the room, and the answers, she was leaving behind.

Kell glared at Juniper. "Do you think we would have gone through all this, if it weren't? Do you think we'd be packing up and heading out to the middle of nowhere if it was all just the delusions of a crazy man?"

"Why now? Why leave now, after all these years?"

They came to a stop. Kell glanced back at her father's room, tears collecting in her eyes. "My dad, he's tired. All those years of fighting it—he's done. The machines don't help anymore anyway. He's going to die."

"Where can you go?"

"There's an uncovered zone not far from here. It's small and most don't even know of its existence. One of those friends my dad mentioned earlier gave him the coordinates for it."

Juniper was stunned. "But, if he goes there…if he dies there, he'll just be gone."

Wiping the tears before they could break free from her lower eyelid, Kell nodded solemnly. "I guess it's better to become nothing, than to suffer forever."

The woman started moving again. "We have to get back to packing. I think…I think it's time for you to go."

Time. Juniper realized she had spent a lot of it inside this woman's house. Her mind raced the couple of blocks back to her own home and to her mother getting ready to commit suicide. She needed to stop Ellen before it was too late.

***

As Juniper approached her house, she could see movement through the front windows. It appeared many of her mother's guests had already arrived.

She slowed her jog to a walk as she reached the front door, the sounds of celebration coming through it. She hoped she wasn't too late.

The living room was crowded. Juniper stood on her toes upon entering to search for Ellen. She couldn't see her from her vantage point, so she started in the direction of the dining room. As she moved through people milling about, a hand fell gently on her shoulder. It was Suze.

"Hey, Juniper. Listen, about the other day—"

Juniper waved dismissively. "Fuck off, Suze."

She recognized most of the people filling her house, but there were a few strangers standing out in the crowd. Juniper figured they were the women from Ellen's weekly breakfast meetings. She had heard plenty of stories about them, but actually never met most of them. Finally, she spotted her mother standing in front of the curio cabinet.

Juniper grabbed Ellen's hand and pulled her away from her guests.

"Juniper, what in the world are you doing?" Ellen tried to give the people around her a reassuring smile.

"Mom, I just came back from—I just..." She didn't know how to say it.

Ellen's face pinched with concern. "Is everything all right?"

Juniper shook her head. She was suddenly very aware of just how many people were within earshot. Even though most of the party guests appeared to be in deep conversation, Juniper couldn't help but notice the way the volume of those conversations had dropped dramatically since she entered the home. No doubt, Suze had already spread her gossip regarding Juniper's revival of Wesley to all who would listen. "Can we go into your room? I really need to talk to you. Now."

Apologizing to her guests for the unexpected intrusion,

Ellen sighed and led the way to her bedroom.

Juniper closed the door behind them.

"Now, are you going to tell me what's going on?"

Juniper opened her mouth to speak, but the words evaporated when she caught sight of the framed photograph lying on top of Ellen's bedspread. Staring through the glass, and from across time, were her parents on their wedding day. Seeing her father's face, Juniper was hit with a horrific understanding. So focused on keeping Ellen from killing herself, she hadn't really thought of her loved ones who were already gone. The realization her dad, and Thomas, had been suffering every second of every day since they died made her want to vomit.

"Juniper, you're starting to scare me."

Swallowing the lump in her throat, Juniper sat on the bed and rested her hand on top of the picture. "Mom, today…today I went to the Walker house and had a talk with old man Walker."

Ellen reeled back as if Juniper just spit on her. "What? Why would you do that? Juniper, those people are crazy."

Glancing at the faces in the photo, Juniper felt her resolve grow. She wouldn't let her mother suffer the same fate as her father. "No, listen, Mom. I went there and talked to them because something was wrong. Ever since that day with Wesley at the fountain, things have been different. I've learned some things…things about Paradise."

Ellen pressed her hand against her forehead. "Juniper, please. I can't take this anymore."

"No, just listen. Gabriel told me—"

"Gabriel?" Ellen cut her off. "Now my daughter is on a first name basis with the Walker family. Wait, you said you went into their house? Did anybody see you?"

"No…I don't know. It doesn't matter. Mom—"

"Oh great! Juniper, what were you thinking?" Ellen

began pacing. "The last thing you want is to be associated with those—"

"Enough! I want you to stop talking and listen to what I have to say!"

Ellen froze, her face a mix of annoyance and something else—fear.

Juniper stood before the woman and told her everything that happened since Wesley nearly drowned. Halfway through, Ellen leaned back against the dresser. It was as if the words she was hearing were so heavy, her legs could not bear the full weight any longer. When Juniper finished, she waited for her mother to speak.

"I just don't know anymore."

Juniper embraced her. "I know. It's so much to take in."

Ellen pushed her away. "No. I don't know about you anymore. What did you think? That this…this wild story would stop me from Ascending?"

Juniper was stunned.

Ellen walked towards the door to the bedroom. "I'll tell you what's happened here. You've been infected by those people. I"—Ellen wiped the tears from her eyes—"I don't want you here. Leave."

"Mom, please, I love you! I'm trying to save you." Juniper could feel her own tears begin to well.

"If you love me, please go. Just for a couple hours, just long enough for me to say good-bye to my friends. I just ask that you leave my grandson here. I want Wesley's face to be the last one I see before I'm reunited with your father."

"No. I'm not leaving, and neither are you."

Juniper stormed past Ellen. The guests in the living room watched as she opened the door, none of them even trying to pretend that they weren't eavesdropping.

"Everybody get the fuck out!" Juniper pointed a finger towards the front door. When nobody immediately moved, she said it again, louder.

Ellen came chasing after her. "Don't listen to her!" Spinning to face her daughter, she added, under her breath so the comment would stay between them, "I swear, I will never forgive you if you ruin this for me."

Juniper nudged past her and headed once again for the dining room. A silver serving platter replaced the usual centerpiece of a white bowl made to resemble coral. Ellen's suicide pills rested in the middle.

Following her, Ellen clawed at her shirt. "Don't you dare!"

Before her mother could stop her, Juniper snatched the pills, ran into the kitchen, and dumped them into the sink. She'd managed to turn on the water before Ellen shoved her out of the way.

"How could you? You selfish little bitch! You won't let me be happy." Ellen tried to salvage the pills.

The scene had grown too uncomfortable for the party guests, most of them taking the opportunity to make themselves scarce. A few still lingered but followed the others when Juniper shifted her gaze on them. Even Suze had the good sense to leave.

With her moment completely ruined, Ellen disappeared into her bedroom, slamming the door behind her. Juniper could hear the woman crying from the other side, but she dared not go in or knock. She believed her mother about not forgiving her—at least in the short term. Juniper could live with it, though. Ellen had to be alive to hate her, and so she would take all the hate the woman could muster.

***

She woke to soft singing. The first few hours after Ellen sequestered herself in her room, Juniper had worried she might try to kill herself during the night, so she'd decided the best place to be was as close to her mother as possible. It meant sleeping on the living room couch. As she sat up and rubbed the sleep from her eyes, she pinged her internal clock. It was nearly six in the morning.

"Mom?"

Ellen was sitting in a nearby rocking chair, her back to Juniper. She was singing a lullaby.

"I found a half of a pill stuck to the edge of the drain. It isn't enough for me, but for a smaller person…"

Confused, Juniper rose off the couch and started across the room.

"I guess it's better this way. Now we can all be together again."

"Mom? What are you talking about?" Juniper felt the sleep leave her body, replaced by a wave of dread.

Cradled in Ellen's arms was Juniper's son, Wesley. The boy appeared to be sleeping.

"Mom!" Juniper wrenched him from her mother. "What have you done?"

"It was the only way. You scared me so badly last night. What if you actually believed all that nonsense? What if you found a way to block yourself—or even worse, Wesley, from the Paradise satellites? You would be lost to me…forever."

Juniper could feel the boy's chest rising and falling, but his breathing was very weak. She let out a moan as she shoved her fingers into his mouth. "C'mon, baby, throw it up."

From the corner of her eye she saw Ellen rise from the chair and retrieve something from under the pillow she had been sitting on. Probably the pill bottle. "Read the directions. See if there's a way to reverse the effects."

"I gave it to him a half hour ago. It's too late, honey. Soon, he'll be in the arms of his father."

Wesley gagged as Juniper continued to ram her fingers as far down his throat as possible, but nothing was coming up. "Please, baby, please, please, please, please."

"Once you see it, once you see Paradise, you'll know everything I do, I do for us. For our family."

"Shut up!"

Juniper, still clutching her son, screamed back towards her mom. "Where's the fucking bottle? Maybe there are instructions on how to stop the process. Or—or a number we can call. Something!"

She turned her attention to the floor and shelves around her. As she searched, she could see the reflection of the entire room in the glass of Ellen's curio cabinet. Even through tear blurred eyes, she could see the knife as it caught the light from a nearby lamp.

"Mom?" Juniper turned just as the blade came at her.

The knife, which would have connected with the side of her neck had she not moved, instead dug into the meat of her bicep. She screamed.

"Please, just let me do it. I'll make it quick!" Ellen jabbed the knife at her a second time.

Juniper intercepted Ellen's arm in mid-attack. She let out a shriek as she wrenched her mother to the floor. The carving knife, jarred from Ellen's grip, slid across the hardwood. Both of them scrambled for it, but Juniper reached it first.

Juniper held the knife between them. "Stop! What the fuck is wrong with you?" She had awoken into a nightmare and was desperate for it to end.

Tears ran down Ellen's face. "Why does it have to be so hard? Why can't you just be a good daughter for once? Why do you want me to suffer?"

Juniper stared at her dying son. Her mother had poisoned him and doomed him to an eternity of torment. Anger flared through her. "You don't know suffering," she said through gritted teeth, "but you will."

***

Juniper stumbled away from her house, Wesley cradled

in her arms. She wanted to look back, but the pain in her arm and the weight of her son prevented her from doing so. The street was empty thanks to the early hour. She moved as fast as she could and soon approached the Walker home. Until the moment she actually saw them out front loading up the moving truck, she had been terrified they would already be gone. "Kell!" Her voice was hoarse and broke near the end, but it was enough. Kell leaned out from the side of the vehicle.

"Juniper?"

When she saw the limp form of the boy in Juniper's arms, she dropped the box she held and rushed over to help.

"What the hell happened?"

With the weight of her son gone, Juniper fell to the ground, wracking sobs sending convulsions through her body. "You have to take us with you."

"I don't understand. What's going on?"

Trying to get her emotions under control, she wiped across her eyes and tilted her head towards the slight form clutched in Kell's arms. "He's dying, Kell. My baby's dying."

"How?"

"My mother, she gave him one of her pills, and he—" She couldn't finish the sentence.

Understanding blossomed across Kell's face. "Did she also do that?" She pointed to Juniper's arm.

"Yes."

Kell peered over Juniper's shoulder at the empty street behind her. "Where is she? Is she chasing you?"

Juniper's chin quivered as she shook her head. "She's… she's where she wants to be."

A moment of silence passed between them as Kell returned her attention to Juniper. "I don't know what you want us to do."

"You have to take us with you, and we need to leave now before—before it's too late."

Kell twisted back to look at her house and the truck out front. Her mouth hung open as she appeared to weigh Juniper's request. "I don't know, hon. It's a bit of a ride, and we don't have a lot of room."

"Please! I can't let him go to Paradise, Kell. I can't let him suffer."

From over by the house came the answer to Juniper's prayers. "It's okay. We'll make room."

Juniper turned to see Gabriel gripping the railing of the porch with frail hands, staring at her.

"Come now, dear, let's get your boy secure."

It was a tight fit, but since Juniper held Wesley on her lap, there was enough room for everybody. As they lifted off the Walker's driveway and started out of the neighbourhood, Juniper caught a glimpse of her house, the front door still open from when she left. She wondered how long it would stay that way.

The morning sun peeked over the trees to the east. It sent a shaft of light across Wesley's face. Juniper slid her fingers through his hair. She prayed they would make it to the uncovered zone in time.

Acknowledgements

The authors would like to thank Michael Drakich, Lori Lorimer, Mick Ridgewell, Write On Windsor, Mirror World Publishing, Kate Richards, Cody Maisonneuve, Justin Cantelo and everybody who helped with the production of this book.

Christian would like to thank his family and friends for putting up with his constant complaining about never having enough time to write. He would also— Oh God, I don't know what happened. I was just in my living room when the sky outside started going crazy. In a flash, I found myself here. The guy who was using this computer looks just like me! Shit, he's coming back from the bathroom, I better hide!—like to thank you for buying this book.

Ben would like to thank his family and friends. You have been hearing me talk about writing since I was a child and I finally put out my first book. Your support through all the years of talking made it easy when I started doing. Many more books will follow, much sooner this time.

Coming Soon from Mirror World Publishing

The Time Traveler's Resort and Museum

David McLain

Chapter 1

Riothamus

When the young man finally came to, an arm was laying at his feet. Not an arm attached to a man, an arm. He wondered whom it belonged to. He shuddered instinctively. He tilted his head back, and a sharp pain struck the back of his head, like a hammer coming down on an anvil. It took him another thirty minutes to stand up. There wasn't any hurry. The battle was over and the Gauls had retreated. The sound of clashing metal had faded; the dead and the dying were left to suffer in peace.

The smell of carrion in the young man's nostrils was overwhelming. He tried to imagine telling his mother about what had happened here. There were things he would never be able to tell her about- the arm, for one, and the smell. How could you explain that to a woman who fed you, clothed you, and cared for you in sickness and health? How could he explain the arm, and the smell, and the pieces of good men that lay all around him? His mother had lost two children already. She never needed to know. No one ever needed to know.

Slowly, painfully, he stood up and surveyed the field. He seemed to be on the far end of the battlefield, though most of the conflict had taken place in the area just east of where he stood. Through the mist he could make out a few women tending to the injured, and a few young boys running back and forth. There had been twelve thousand men on the field that day. The young man had never seen so many men at once- in fact, no one had, it was the largest assembly of men for any purpose since the Romans had left Britain. How many were left now on his side? On any side?

Before the young man had lost consciousness, the numbers appeared to have thinned out to eight or nine hundred. He surveyed the field again. It was difficult to tell how many were still standing.

Slowly, he lurched forward toward the center of the field. There was a sharp pain in his ankle and he limped on his left leg. 'The battle is over,' he reminded himself. 'The battle is over, and the Gauls have retreated. The King will be King of everything south of Hadrian's Wall, at least for now, and I will be able to go home. I'll go home and all of this will be over. I'll go hunting, and fishing, and riding. Mother will cook for me. I'll dance with pretty girls underneath a silver moon. I'll go home, and all of this will be behind me. It is all over now.'

He lifted his legs over the field of trampled grass, doing his best to find a path around the piles of flesh that littered the field. A dying horse looked up at him. Its belly was slit open and a bone fragment was sticking out of its left foreleg. The eyes of the horse turned gray as his neck twitched. The young man turned away and shuddered. He kept walking forward, through the fog toward the east. There had been some kind of town over there; a fishing village or something. If he could get there, everything would be all right. He just had to get there.

He almost ran into the young boy before he saw him. He had seen him somewhere before, in the fields, or maybe at a banquet, he wasn't really sure. They were only three or four years apart in age- under other circumstances they might have gone fishing together, or gone out with some girls and gotten drunk late at night on a beach. The boy didn't seem to be injured. He looked frantic, as if they had been looking for each other for a long time. The young man wondered if he looked as desperate as the boy before him did.

"Glædne heahfrea," the boy said.

'How can he call me that?' The young man wondered. 'Isn't there anyone else?' But of course, the look in the boy's eyes answered his question before even he had time to ask it. 'No, there isn't anyone else. That's why he looks so happy to see me. He's been looking for hours and I'm the first he's found. Everybody else is dead. That's why he's here. He's looking for you, expecting you to know what to do. The King-' the young man's train of thought suddenly derailed. He looked at the boy's eyes and almost instantly understood.

"Rioðamus?" He asked.

The boy ran a hand through his short, brown hair and scratched the back of his neck. The young man nodded and closed his eyes. The back of his head was killing him. When he opened his eyes, he saw that the boy had turned around again and was walking back toward the opposite end of the field. "Cwom wit mē" the boy said, and he turned around and trudged back across the field.

Rioðamus- The River King. The Greatest King. If ever anyone had deserved the title it would be him. It was his love of his men that had been his greatest strength, and they had returned the favor with the title. To him all men, great and small, were like long lost brothers. He could talk to the poorest beggar and the highest Lord with equal aplomb; everyone felt like he was their friend, like their problems were his. Even though he was King, he remembered the name of every man he'd ever shaken hands with. He would remember their names, and the names of their family. He wasn't what you expected a king to be. He had a wicked sense of humor and was known to tell the dirtiest jokes of anyone in the country. He was noble too, and brave, and kind. It was hard to accept that now- all that was over. Now, everything was over. The young man tried to push that thought out of his mind. 'Resignation,' he thought. 'That's understandable. You have to do what needs to be done, and after that we'll see.'

The young man and the boy trudged forward in silence. Slowly, but surely they made their way over the field and into the small town that they had just finished defending. The young man wondered what the name of it was. It wasn't much of a town, really just a few ramshackle stone cottages thrown together on a small strip of land between water and beach. As they walked past, frightened women quickly shut the doors and shutters on the small stone cottages. Playing in the mud, a group of small, dirty faces stared up at them. The young man could hear the sound of the ocean roaring far away. In the distance he saw an abbey on top of a small hill. They would have brought him there. Somehow the young man knew that at this point there was nothing else that could be done for him.

They found their way almost effortlessly. The young man and the boy climbed the hill to the abbey, where a woman met them at the stones steps of the church. She stood there, mute, a serene expression on her face, neither moving nor speaking as they approached. She was lovely, but her feet were bare and there was a wild, feral look about her, like a child raised by wolves. Her hair was pitch black, and cascaded down her shoulders in ringlets. The boy looked at her, and nodded before turning around and heading back toward the field of battle. She stared at him passively. Her eyes revealed neither pride nor shame.

'She's beautiful' the young man thought, shocked at the random, scattered thoughts that popped in and out of his mind. 'She's beautiful. The king is dead. We fought a war today. The Gauls retreated. I will get to go home again. I can never go home again. She's beautiful. I need to hold on.'

"Þā cyning?" The young man asked. (The King?)

"Þā cyning is nēah, "she said as calmly as if he had asked her about the weather. "Cwom."

They turned around and walked through the chapel. The young man thought about saying a prayer, but he couldn't think of what to say. The chapel was small, and hard, and gray. The young woman faced a statue of the Virgin Mary and bowed her head. The young man took a moment, and stared at the floor, before walking out into the back room of the church.

It didn't seem like a place for a king to die. He lay there on a simple stretcher, with no more ceremony than a common soldier might have. His beard was bloody and his arms looked disjointed, but he didn't look like he was dying. Maybe it would be all right. It was difficult to tell. The young man knelt down beside him. The smell was overwhelming. 'The smell of death,' he thought. 'I have to pretend. I have to pretend I don't smell it. Just look at him. He looks fine. Just look at him.' The young man looked at the King's face and tried to smile. The King opened his eyes and stared at him.

"Hwæt!" he said. He spoke with a small laugh, as if all of this were a practical joke on him. "Adam," he said. The young man nodded. He had never been sure why it was that the King called him that. It wasn't his name. Normally he would object, but of course things like that didn't matter just now. With a great effort, the King raised his hand to his chest. It was only then that the young man noticed the sword.

The King's beautiful sword was still clutched in his left hand; or rather, the hilt of his sword was still in his hand. The blade had shattered, leaving only a small stub where the deadliest weapon in Britain had once been. The cold flat steel of the hilt was still perfect, but its power was gone now, gone forever. It had shattered like a chicken bone, or an old piece of wood.

"Wē wunne," the King said.

"Wē wunne," The young man repeated.

"Ond min deað," The King gasped.

"No," the young man said firmly, as if his insistence would be enough. The king laughed again.

"Nū morgen," The King said. "Nū cyning. Ic Fæder fæþmum, ond Ic spræce mit mitig."

And with that, he died.

***

They buried the King at the abbey. He was laid in the hollow of an oak tree, near the men who had died so willingly protecting his kingdom and his throne. The hilt of his sword was laid on his chest. The young man had a local blacksmith lay down the engraving on the hilt, so that the world would know him for all time. It was nothing extravagant, just a simple dedication in Latin. The plot was marked with a stone pyramid and nothing more. The funeral was attended by the men who had survived, and those who were there were convinced that he would have been honored. He was now the past, and the future.

A new morning. A new king. I embrace the Father and I speak with might.

Those were his last words, and they haunted the young man until he became an old man, long after the old king had become a myth and a shadow. When the young man was asked about the old king, and he was asked more times than he could remember, he would usually talk about his love of the people, of all people, and the way he could make men laugh. But sometimes, just sometimes, when it was late at night, he would tell people about the last words of the king, and the engraving the blacksmith had put on the sword:

HIC IACET
ARTHVR

Christian Laforet lives in LaSalle, Ontario with his wife, Lady, and his two girls, Lelaina Blue and Delilah Sunshine. For more info about Christian and his work, go to ChristianLaforet.com

Ben Van Dongen was born in Windsor Ontario and currently lives on the thin line that separates that city from LaSalle. Not being qualified to become an Astronaut, he decided to write science fiction as a way of showing up those who are. His delusions continue unabated. This is his first book. BenVanDongen.com

CPSIA information can be obtained
at www.ICGtesting.com
Printed in the USA
LVOW12s0058230916

505838LV00001B/2/P